I'm Zombie

A Zombie Mosaic novel

I'm Zombie

A Zombie Mosaic novel

Tony Newton

COSMIC
EGG
BOOKS

Winchester, UK
Washington, USA

First published by Cosmic Egg Books, 2016
Cosmic Egg Books is an imprint of John Hunt Publishing Ltd., Laurel House, Station Approach,
Alresford, Hants, SO24 9JH, UK
office1@jhpbooks.net
www.johnhuntpublishing.com

For distributor details and how to order please visit the 'Ordering' section on our website.

Text copyright: Tony Newton 2015

ISBN: 978 1 78535 096 2
Library of Congress Control Number: 2015934341

A CIP catalogue record for this book is available from the British Library.

Design: Stuart Davies

Printed in the USA by Edwards Brothers Malloy

We operate a distinctive and ethical publishing philosophy in all
areas of our business, from our global network of authors to
production and worldwide distribution.

Dedicated to: My wife, Kerry, my Son Reece,
Mum and Dad and to all the preppers
and survivors across the globe!

Accounts from the Zombie Apocalypse — letters, notes, documents, chatroom and forum fragments.

"Beware; for I am fearless, and therefore powerful."
Mary Shelley, *Frankenstein*

Documents found after Z–one (usually referred to as World War Three).

The new Plague hit everyone. No one was safe from its evil clutches. I was too young to really understand what happened or to be fully aware of the danger that was surrounding all of us. The world we live in now, is all I really know.

I live in Ittoqqortoormiit, Greenland. The town used to have over 450 residents before the Zombie War; now we have 38. Most people carry scars mentally and physically from the day the virus spread across the globe.

Everyone remembers October the 10th 2019.

The day the dead outnumbered the living!

Private emails from Meddza corp.

Ref: MeddzaMemo/zero/z
Date: 9th October 2019
From: Dr. P. Channandra President of MEDDZA-CORP

MEMORANDUM

Att: Meddza employees

Re: Vaccine

I would like to thank each employee who has offered themselves and members of their family as test subjects in the trials of Ari-flu and Brenza. The results have been far better than we could have anticipated. We will be rolling out the vaccine as soon as possible.

This information is sensitive and for employees of MEDDZA only.

For the first wave of the vaccine we have allocated one thousand units in total. This may seem insufficient but each and every member of staff will receive the vaccine. There have been nine hundred red cards issued to key personnel. They will receive the vaccine first. Following on from the initial distribution we will be providing green cards, hopefully within the next few weeks. We aim to have fifty thousand vaccines dispensed within one to three weeks and we hope to be issuing the vaccine to citizens across the country as soon as possible. This will be a challenging task but we have every confidence that we will be able to fulfil these orders.

I understand that some of you are currently working in terrible conditions. I would like to reassure you that we are striving to rectify this as soon as we possibly can. I also understand that some of you are in desperate need of certain supplies, including food and drink. We are doing our best to meet all requirements as quickly as possible.

Thank you for your patience on this.

Please only contact me directly if you are no longer able to contact your local officer.

Thank you all for signing a non-disclosure agreement regarding these trials.

Please be aware that the trials were carried out in the strictest confidence.

I cannot stress this enough!

Best Regards,

Dr. P.Channandra

Line–7626

Ref: MeddzaMemo/zero/z

Date: 10th October 2019

From: Dr. P. Channandra President of MEDDZA-CORP

MEMORANDUM

Att: Meddza employees

Re: Vaccine Distribution

We are very excited and blessed to be announcing that we are currently distributing a vaccine. I would like to give thanks to all of our wonderful and hard-working employees, who really have gone the extra mile.

It is my great pleasure to have been asked to personally thank every member of staff by the President of the United States of

America, the Prime Minister of Britain and the Royal families across the globe.

You will be receiving your shipments of Brenza and Ari-flu later today. Please only supply to the appropriate red card holders. No replacements can or will be issued to any faculty. No damaged or lost doses will be replaced. We are taking precautions and using heavily guarded vans during transportation to ensure safe delivery. In certain areas the stock will be delivered via helicopter. You will be informed of the drop off points as soon as we have that information.

Please issue vaccines swiftly to prevent queuing, as this may cause risk to both parties. Please do not attempt to steal any of the stock for family or friends, though we do understand that it may be tempting to do so and that this is a situation that none of us imagined we would have to face. However, each and every phial is accounted for. As you were previously informed, every employee will receive one dose. It is the choice of the employee and card holders to distribute this as they see fit. If you wish to give your quota to a family member, this is allowed. But we recommend that every person who is allocated the vaccine takes it. Staff may rest assured that more will soon be available for the general public. We are ready to safely distribute. Security will be in full operation at all times.

Please only contact me directly if you can no longer contact your local officer.

Best Regards,

Dr. P. Channandra

Line–7626

Ref: Meddza Memo/zero/z
Date: 10th October 2019
From: Dr.P.Channandra   President of MEDDZA-CORP

MEMORANDUM

Att: Meddza employees

Re: Vaccine Reactions

We have received reports of adverse reactions to the Ari-flu and Brenza vaccines. Please distribute this information to your team immediately.

Please report any incidents to your local officer or myself. This could provide vital information and help save lives.

The reports of adverse reactions we have received are primarily from the elderly and subjects on long-term medication. There is nothing to worry about if your vaccine has already been administered. However, as a precautionary measure we are ceasing distribution and administration of Air Flu and Brenza for the time being.

Report any adverse effects immediately, making sure to include the following details:

Patient Name
Patient's full medical history
Location
Isolate ID
Patient status
Last vaccinated
Specimen source
Any Treatment given
Date of Treatment given
Your Institute information

Please quarantine any patient appearing to have adverse reactions to the drugs.

Please only contact me directly if you can no longer contact your local officer.

Best Regards,

Dr. P. Channandra

Line–7626

Ref: Meddza Memo/zero/z
Date: 11th October 2019
From: Dr. P. Channandra President of MEDDZA-CORP

MEMORANDUM

Att: Meddza employees

Re: Important Vaccine Information

Any unused Ari-flu and Brenza vaccines should be destroyed. This decision has not been taken lightly, it is with much regret, but the safety of our members of staff and red card holders is of the highest priority. Please do not panic.

Be sure to report any adverse reactions to myself or an officer immediately and quarantine the patients.

We are working on another vaccine twenty-four/seven and each patient report we receive will help us to fine tune and move this process along as swiftly as possible.

My deepest sympathies go out to our offices and units in England, Australia, and the United States of America. We have lost over seventy-five employees, as well as very large number of patients, VIPs and other key personnel from around the world, including voluntary workers.

The secretary, CFO, and COO of MEDDZA have been air-lifted to a medical facility by helicopter and are receiving treatment. My prayers are with them and their families at this sad time.

Please only contact me directly if you can no longer contact your local officer.

Best Regards,

Dr. P. Channandra

Line–7626

Notes found in central London October 2019.

October the 12th 2019

My name is Dr Simon Rosenbaum,

Until recently I worked as a scientist for MEDDZA, the well-known pharmaceutical giant. MEDDZA was the largest pharmaceutical organization in the world and was previously funded by the government. My job was interesting, to say the least. From time to time, I would hear rumours, always unsubstantiated, of scientists employed by MEDDZA disappearing. The things we worked on were highly classified government secrets and it was fairly common knowledge that MEDDZA would stop at nothing to ensure that information didn't fall into the wrong hands. I worked hard and I was trustworthy. Although I was good at my job, I think I may have been victim to some tests of loyalty in the past. I received offers from other companies, for information about advanced medicines that we were working on, promising the kind of money that could instantly buy a house most people can only dream about. Suspect or not – I declined. I wasn't in it solely for the money. I gave one hundred and ten per cent at all times and put in extra hours when I could. I assumed that they knew I was more committed and honest than most.

I've had many jobs in the past but this was the only one that I had to be micro-chipped for (like a pet). It didn't hurt but I could feel it under the surface of my skin. I used to think that the chip contained poison, and that they could kill me with the press of a button, or maybe, if I were to travel out of range (perhaps a flight to Russia) to sell my secrets, the chip would explode, like a bomb. I'm of the belief that this tiny piece of plastic was what stopped many of the greedier and money hungry scientists selling out to other countries or organisations.

I chose to work there; I loved the job. The salary was just an added bonus; after all, I was getting paid for doing something I loved. The amount I earned made a heart surgeon's income look small.

We worked on projects that could have easily destroyed the entire planet within a matter of hours. I was one of only a handful of scientists, globally, capable of developing this type of biochemical weapon. We kept some of them stored on the premises, protected by armed guards twenty-four/seven. It was hard for me not to have a god complex. I had created these concoctions which could end life as we knew it, and I could use them if I chose to (not that I would – but it was bizarre having that much power).

Picking the wrong person for this job wasn't an option and we were carefully vetted. But, no matter how hard they tried, things can change people: relationships, family and experiences. Suppose the scientist in charge of a project developing a lethal virus, found out that his wife was cheating on him? One day he walked in to his perfect home life and discovered it was all a lie; all he had known and loved had been stolen from him. He goes off to work and doesn't want to live anymore ... or the scientist who discovers he has cancer and thinks, why should anyone deserve to live! BOOM! It's all over. It's too much power for anyone to have. Most of the things I created were never seen again, the government (I assume) kept them for defence purposes. Just imagine a threat from another country, like Hiroshima, we could be wiped out within an instant.

Watching anyone die is horrific, knowing it's final, it's the end and you'll never get the chance to speak to or hug that person again. Watching your friends and work colleagues suffer right in front of you is sheer terror. I couldn't help them and I felt useless. Nothing could have prepared me for what my eyes have seen. The internet and phone systems are down, everything is down. Why the decision was never made by the government to end the suffering before it even began, I will never know. I know they had the power to do that! Maybe it's not time, maybe this was planned? I can't do anything but guess.

I write this by candlelight, using the electric lighting is too much of a risk. I don't want to attract anyone, infected or otherwise.

Inside of this lab, as far as I know, I am the only one alive. I have run out of food and have very little to drink. I thought I was one of the lucky ones to survive this far but I was wrong. Watching it happen around me and not being able to do anything to help, seeing my friends and colleagues slowly starve, is not lucky at all.

The corpses around me coming back to life was like something from a horror film and I've seen some bizarre things in my time! None of us could control it. We didn't think that we would get infected but blood runs through the corridors where we would once chat over coffee and make small talk about what was on TV and complain about the weather. This place is swarming with the undead. You can hear them throwing themselves against the doors; the continual thumps are like a clock, counting down to that moment that they break through. The screaming has stopped now but the incessant moaning continues. The lack of screams confirms to me that there are no survivors.

I have seen security guards, co-workers, police and even members of the army being eaten alive, torn limb from limb. I've watched those infected with the virus change into a ghost of their former selves. I should have noticed that the executives were nowhere to be seen (probably in a bunker somewhere), they were long gone. I and another employee were the highest ranking and therefore in charge, though no one was in charge of this horrendous mess.

I was so close, who knows, maybe I still am. The company tried to rush things for a big payday, but what use is money now? The first vaccine was good enough as a standard anti-viral and would have stood up to even the most virulent of diseases. It should have had some effect on the infected patient but it did nothing! I think they had to give out something, in a way; they needed to look as if they were giving all the important people something at least – even if it was only hope – in exchange for a pile of money. Now I am our last hope. As far as I am aware, every single one of our base facility testing centres has been compromised. The problem is that we got eager too soon. We thought we had a vaccine, but we were wrong.

Even if someone succeeds in finding a drug that actually works – is it already too late? I think it is! Just before communication completely broke down, there were rumours of cases of immunity from all stages of the virus, including the second stage – a manifestation of rabid, zombie like symptoms! From videos I have seen online, no one seems to bypass the first stage onset of basic, flu like symptoms, so at least there is some warning – a red light – if people are in the company of someone turning, that at least gives them a few minutes to get the hell away from the infected! Better still, if they have the stomach and a weapon to hand, to put them down like the walking plague they are. There must be something, some way to provide immunity to the bites, the infection that they carry. Nothing has worked so far – but there has to be a cure.

I have a decision to make. I can either die of starvation alone here, or walk out into the thick of it and take my chances after injecting myself with a phial of the newest trial vaccine. When you have nothing to lose, you have nothing to fear. My latest vaccine hasn't been tested. I don't know how close, if at all, I am.

The thought that haunts me is – could I have saved everyone? Was time the only factor that prevented me from ending this horror? Was I, or maybe one of my fellow workmates, the cause of this evil plague? If even one per cent of me thought for a millisecond that I might be responsible for unleashing this terrible infection on humanity, I would have made it my mission to find a gun, press it to my temple and pull the trigger. Who knows, maybe it will come to that soon enough.

I need more time to construct thorough tests on the vaccine but there is no one here to use as a test subject, willing or otherwise! There are only the dead – or the undead now.

Only those who were torn limb from limb and eaten alive didn't resurrect. I've seen brains and intestines pulled from peoples' bodies and ravenously devoured by the pack of undead, like dogs fighting over a piece of meat.

I have the means to wipe out millions of people in an instant. But how can I be sure that there are no survivors of this thing out there? I don't want the deaths of innocent people on my hands. I only want to destroy the infected. Who am I to make this decision? I'm no God. I'm a nobody. I try to believe that this won't be the end for civilization, that pockets of people will survive, we, as a race, are born survivors. Will things ever be the same? No – I don't think they ever will. But it doesn't take a genius to work that out. Still I cling to the idea that this will not be the end – only a new chapter. This is our World War III, only this time, who knows, we may all get along afterwards. No more fighting other countries for oil, food, money, status. Greed – it may all just go out of the window. We will have one thing in common – we will all have lost loved ones, watched people die, watched them suffer and not been able to do a damn thing to help them. But, yes, there will be some kind of civilisation. We are an amazing race; every day we cure something. Okay, the general public don't know the half of it, but we can cure almost anything, or at least, we could, before. It might have cost millions to do so, and you wouldn't have found this stuff on the National Health Service, but it was out there. The thing is, if every disease was cured, everyone would live to around a 110 years of age and the world would be dangerously overpopulated. Why then, with all those great resources, didn't the powers that be have plans in place for a situation like this? Why did they not look at Swine Flu as a warning, or Ebola! Increasingly, viruses were mutating and growing stronger. This, I'm afraid to say, was inevitable.

In the past, I have constructed deadly diseases and viruses. Thankfully, this doesn't look like one of my own; at least I don't have that on my conscience! Maybe it is something I, or a colleague, discovered that has now mutated. I can't be certain that it's not. Maybe it's a beast made by another country, who knows? Maybe it's been there the whole time, just lying dormant, waiting for the right conditions to mutate. Maybe we have been carriers all along, just waiting for the spark to ignite it!

What will I miss?

I will miss everything, my family and friends, my job, the rain, the sun, and the view from my bedroom window. I can honestly say that I have loved every minute of my existence and I wouldn't change a thing. Luckily, the good has always outweighed the bad in my life and you can't get a better deal than that. I would have done some things differently, of course. I think I would have had a meaningful relationship (I put it off – like most of us who get side tracked by our careers). I know I have saved more lives than I have unwittingly taken, even though I have developed deadly viruses that may or may not have been used in wars across the globe. I'm grateful though that I'll never know if anyone has died from the weapons I have designed in this room. The reason I made them was to protect us, and I hope anything that I have made was used only for that purpose.

The dead who have turned and entered the secondary stage of infection cannot be treated, there's no going back at this stage. With time, maybe they would enter a vegetative state, and perhaps have the ability to learn, but either way, they would never, mentally, resemble their former self. Engineering this vegetative state would be playing God, literally. I hope it doesn't ever go down that route. As of now, nothing works on them. I have killed six of them so far. I have performed tests and you have to totally destroy the brain when they are in the second stage of infection. Only this will kill them. My experiments have shown that brain parasites can be ruled out. Therefore I must assume that this was man-made. It is unlike anything I have seen previously.

The virus starts like a flu, eating at your immune system, weakening you until your body can't take any more. The onset of symptoms takes place very quickly, sometimes within minutes of being infected/bitten. It's like experiencing all the symptoms of the worst strain of super-flu. Imagine having super-flu with the shakes, a temperature that is off the scale, delirium, and a headache that makes a migraine seem pleasant. As the virus multiplies, your blood feels like its boiling, your airways are closing up and every part of your body is under attack. There is, however, a difference in the rate of turning. It would appear that the young and healthy have better resistance and take longer to succumb to the second stage than the old or those who have an immune deficiency or underlying illness. The ill and infirm cannot fight the disease for very long, but to be honest, these people are the lucky ones. They will not have to suffer for a protracted length; it may be only a matter of minutes or even seconds. But so dreadful is the disease that those minutes would seem like hours that never end.

Perhaps this virus has mutated with another to cause these devastating effects.

Prevention is going to be the key (here comes my part) though I think it is long past the prevention stage! The government received immediate information on what was happening. The time for action was short – this thing spreads like wildfire. But it should have been sufficient time for contingency plans to be put in place. My thoughts keep returning to the idea that I may have the cure! I am the only test subject here. The zombies – (the infected humans) – will rot eventually if nothing is done to them. I assume this will take a while. But rot they will. The last official report that I heard confirmed that the plague has spread all over the globe, from major cities to tiny villages; everywhere has reported a virus with similar effects.

There were teams of scientists and specialists (just like us here) spread around the world, the largest test centre located in the United States. Before communications failed, we were sharing our reports between one another, in the hopes of finding a cure faster, or at least, finding a cure. It seemed everyone exposed had the same reaction to the virus, give or take a small difference in time frame, from when they became infected to when they first began to show symptoms. Animals have not displayed any sign of the secondary stage of the virus, displaying only the initial onset symptoms, similar to standard influenza. In humans, when the secondary stage hits the brain, vital signs cease and to all intents and purposes, the victim is physically dead. Then, with a jolt (almost as if Dr Frankenstein himself had attached electrodes emitting an electrical pulse to the brain, an aberrant form of life returns; a zombie like state where, although there is no pulse and breathing no longer takes place, the infected arise to become flesh eating monsters, who no longer resemble their former selves.

Those infected showing secondary stages of the virus do not need to drink and do not need to eat to exist. Yet they seem motivated to do so! Their internal organs are useless; they cannot digest food properly, so they are constantly craving flesh. They will not excrete bodily waste, they will have no memories, they don't have the ability to heal, they will not need to sleep, the heart no longer controls the body; I have seen secondary stage victims' bodies, with the heart removed, still moving and walking. The brain itself is infected. They are simply predators.

I cannot work out why they crave human flesh, perhaps they

have regressed back to primal instincts? The zombies do seem to retain an awareness of the difference between those, like themselves, who are undead and those who are still living. Their preferred choice is for warm, living flesh, rather than dead meat, but I assume that, forced to, they will devour the dead in time. So far, I have only witnessed them feeding on the living. I have never seen them touch cold flesh, animal flesh or any other food source.

They are constantly hungry, even the ones that have their intestines ripped out or hanging from their bodies!

My head is pounding. I'm finding it hard to concentrate.

I wonder why it is, even though the brain itself is damaged or destroyed in some way, that they do not try to attack one another? The virus takes over the host body as if it was an empty shell, wiping out all recollection of any previous existence. They appear to have no memory, and from what I can make out, they do not recognise each other. The only motivation remaining to them is centred on biting and feasting. They exist now in a rabid state, their eyes bloodshot, the veins prominent. Most have oozing cuts and sores.

Through my observations and experimentation, I can definitively state that tranquilizers and morphine have no effect at all. Their blood can be dangerous and it is advisable to take steps to ensure you do not get it in your mouth or in open wounds or your eyes.

The first stage of the virus is now airborne, this became obvious due to the rapid rate at which it was spreading. There are no known cases of immunity. The disease is relentless and merciless. Anyone, of any age and of either gender, who has been infected will turn into one of these creatures.

I'm beginning to feel increasingly unwell. I have a headache behind my right eye. I am trying to make myself believe that it is down to a lack of sleep. I have been working solidly now for over twenty-four hours, with mainly coffee with plenty of sugar to keep me going. Still, I fear that time for me is running out.

The vaccine itself (if it works) will be useless unless it is used in a controlled situation, when all the living dead have been removed. Otherwise, there remains the possibility that they may attack, kill you and devour your flesh, and, if the inoculation worked, you would not turn. If you managed to escape with your life, you would, in all likelihood, bleed to death from the bite wound before being able to access medical help. Nor would there be any point in issuing a working vaccine without the control of law and order in place. Nothing can stop stage two infected people from biting. They would need to be killed or removed first.

God knows, the government should not have let it get to this stage at all. Back-up plans should have been in place from the very start. Their sloppy mistakes have cost thousands, if not millions, of lives already. I have no way of distributing the drug even if it does work, and no means for mass production. There is only enough vaccine here for one or two. At best it will save me from getting the virus and turning into one of those things. But it won't stop them from eating my brains or save me from getting shot in the head by a gang of looting survivors.

I have injected the phial (#Z-327) into my system. I'm alive, although I still don't know if I am now immune to the virus or if it will prevent the second stage (turning into a zombie). I'm going to take my findings and this briefcase and leave. My hope is that it works and that I can get it to someone who can take it further and use it to save humanity. I hope I make it.

I have faith – and that is all I need at this time.

"I, at any rate, am convinced that He (God) does not throw dice." – Albert Einstein

Simon Rosenbaum (Dr)

Archived online chat room from the day of the outbreak October the 10th 2019.

(GMT Standard Time)

<Guest5>: Hi what the hell is going on? The police are everywhere, but they are not saying a word, I have seen men in what appear to be gas masks and hazmat suits, something big is going down out there...

<markMod>: Hi where are you?

<Guest5>: Hi there, I'm in the UK, on the outskirts of the city of London.

<markMod>: I would stay indoors Guest5! It could be a terrorist attack or even a chemical spillage.

<Guest5>: cheers

<markMod>: It makes a change getting something serious and off topic on here, this is an online gaming chat room, a kind of chill out room after the eyes are starting to seize up from screen burn!

<Guest1>: Holy shit, there are armed forces here out in the streets too. They are telling us to move away from the city, but giving no explanation. I assume it is a terrorist attack, got to get the hell out of here now, no more gaming for me today.

<markMod>: This is really strange, nothing here; I'm in New Jersey – as yet anyway.

<Guest5>: It's not just me then! I thought I was going mad or something. People in London are always rushing about and would not stop even if a car was on fire or someone was getting mugged in front of them.

<Guest3>: Listening to the radio here! It did say something about a flu epidemic imminent! Big cities like London will need to take precautions first! Just think of the volume of people touching those escalators railings, rubbing their eyes, putting

their fingers in their mouths and breathing in other people's germs. And the tube itself – packed like cattle in rush hour!

<Guest3>: This is rather strange – reports are coming in on the news and on the radio here in the UK and the people on the TV the newscasters look worried as hell they look shook up and scared!

<Guest64>: What are the symptoms?

<Guest5>: The symptoms may include sudden onset fever, chills and aching, lethargy, runny nose, coughing, coughing up blood, nose bleeds and vomiting.

<Guest3>: No shit guys it is a zombie outbreak, have you seen all the footage of the cannibal attacks it's to strange! No this is not some weird role play or a joke, this is a zombie outbreak. There is a video up from the middle east of people turning from their death beds now into zombies...

<Guest5>: Zombies! I don't think so! You must watch too many TV programs and films! Are you a conspiracy theorist by any chance!

<markMod>: This must be a joke...

<Guest3>: No this is real guys I', no conspiracy nut just look around you! what the fuck......

<markMod>: No this does seem to be legit. I have just seen the news damn that was quick every news station is covering the same story, the dead rise, this really is it, well it is really happening. I'm going to go get my daughter from school stay safe guys whatever it is, I hope it's just scare tactics or a joke but I'm not taking chances and you lot should not either.

<Guest9>: Cannibal pics and videos are appearing on popular tube sites as I type this!!

<Guest3>: No shit! Good luck try to stay safe.

<markMod>: This is from a website online "mystery flu outbreak causes mass destruction globally", what will be the effect on economics.

This is officially on the CDC website, it seems pretty vague and about standard influenza.

Influenza – Urgent information.

This leaflet contains important information to keep you safe.

CITIZENS FOR DISEASE CONTROL

Urgent contacts:

CDC 08080-1234-912456

United Kingdom – Dial – 0-999

United States of America – Dial – 0-911

www.citizensfordiseasecontrol.com

Please read all of the information you have received if you hold a current passport/driver's license or you are registered to vote.

Why are you receiving this and what makes this form of flu so different?

Influenza (commonly known as the flu virus) has been around for many years, but we are beginning to see a change with Swine Flu and with the current virulent strain. We are taking extra precautions, as well as providing to date advice. Pandemic flu spreads at a rapid rate from person to person.

The current new form of influenza means that anyone can be at risk:

–Adults and children, both healthy and those with existing health problems.

–The elderly and pregnant women.

All flu viruses are most commonly spread through droplets (tiny particles) in the air. If you come into contact with these invisible droplets you stand at risk of becoming infected by anyone already infected with the influenza virus. The flu virus is passed on in many ways. If someone is suffering from the virus and they cough or sneeze onto their hand, whatever they touch next will also be contaminated and remain so for up to 24 hours.

BE AWARE FLU CAN SPREAD FAST

If you think that you or a member of your family may have the influenza virus, please contact your local GP or hospital to register your symptoms.

Symptoms of influenza are:
–High temperature
–Hot/cold sweats (shivering)
–Aches and pains in muscles and joints
–Cough
–Sore throat
–Headache
–Runny nose/sneezing
–Nose bleed
–Blood present in mucous
–Irritated eyes
–Petechial rash
–Abdominal pain
–Loss of appetite
–Nausea
–Vomiting

Complications of this strain of influenza may also include heart failure and pneumonia. Dial your country code then 09007771248111 immediately if you are showing any of these symptoms.

If you have recently made plans to travel abroad please check with your Travel Company or foreign office for updates.

<Guest5>: No Vaccine!! That's about right ey. What they are thinking about bloody saving money that's what the evil parasitic bastards.

<Guest27>: On the official CDC website it is saying that there is no FDA approved treatment or vaccine, this is very worrying

if it does spread further.

The above piece is not from the official CDC website that is for sure "Citizens for disease Control is either a hoax website or a new one set up solely for this!!!

<Guest12>: Well enough of reading this crap, I'm going to play World War Heroes on the pc, better than listening to this drivel.

<Guest5>: Is this mutated Ebola, Bird flu or even a science experiment gone wrong?

<Guest9>: That is crazy just noticed the Citizens part on the writing!!!! CDC my arse! Looks like someone just wasted some of their precious time!

There were rumors from the Pentagon last year saying they Knew a zombie outbreak was imminent,, it said they were prepared to face the zombie apocalypse, the same article mentioned that the US was not the only country prepared for a zombie outbreak and that the Up was also well prepared and strongly defended other than these two reports and the old CDC website with their comedy (well it seemed comedy at the time) sheet on how to stay alive in the zombie apocalypse I have not heard of anything, this shit is going down – the zombie apocalypse is here!

<Guest23>: It's on the news saying this virus is deadly looks like a plague flu shot on the cards! they are saying they are unclear of the side effects scary shit really, well I have none of the symptoms so at least I'm fine.

<Guest14>: Is the government covering something else up? Are they playing the flu virus down? Or has this been created to cover up another problem?

Officials are saying that this is the most widespread flu epidemic in history.

<Guest17>: If I get it: I'm going to kill myself immediately! I will not end up a monster trying to kill my own flesh and blood.

<Guest23>: Can you post the video for us; it won't be as boring as listening to this bullshit. (Only Joking, I'm off to play some

more shoot me ups hays.)

<Guest14>: My partner is a health freak, he never gets ill. He eats only clean food raw and unprocessed. He has gone down with a flu today. He could not even get out of the bed. I'm now worried he may have this. I feel sick.

<Guest7>: Wow my god I have just seen one of them I almost shit myself, I thought it was a joke, bugger this it is real the policeman just put thirty shells into it took that many for it to go down. My advice acquire a gun now.

<Guest9>: I'm off this is real, good luck out there!

<Guest24>: Anyone wants to cam to cam chat??? Well it is the end of the world! No men please, only women, you have to be fit and be around 18 -30, no sod it It's the end of the world female and a pulse will do!

<Guest15>: Oh Jesus this is not a joke.

<Guest7>: Government and health experts have today revealed that they are struggling to contain the recent super flu outbreak officials are saying the virus is spreading at an uncontrollable rate which we are struggling to keep under control but have announced that they will do everything in their power to progress in the right direction providing the correct medical care. At present they estimate a three month time frame to fully bring the current epidemic under control...

<Guest17>: You may be in luck guest 24, you may find a zombie willing to chat with you, no one human would, and the people you normally go for don't have a brain cell let alone a brain!

<Guest20>: There are zombies everywhere here! they walk slowly, but fuck me are they scary!

<Guest5>: I have been asked to leave. I have to go, I have been asked to take personal belongs like phones and passports and wallets that is all. No change of clothes. This is freaking me out. I'm so scared.

<Guest7>: Get out of the city or any busy populated areas, I

have been told this from my father in the US.

<Guest29>: I killed one, he was in the middle of turning, and it died from a puncture to its heart, I did not have to destroy its brain though I was lucky I think it died because it was turning into one from the virus or death or whatever is gung on inside the.

<Guest5>: Find a safe location and stay there.

<Guest5>: There is a huge military presence we are being forced out of our homes here.

<Guest5>: All schools are now officially closed. Including colleges. And higher education.

<Guest29>: Guest 5 –can't be all bad then.

<Guest5>: This is not a joke, this is the text from a video doing the rounds online from the President of the United States– this is his official response to this outbreak.

"I firstly want to thank the citizens of America for volunteering their services and for contributing to the efforts of the Armed Forces and the Medical services. I am proud of Americans on this day. This is an update on the terrible occurrences we are experiencing. I can assure you that we are putting all our efforts into tackling the problem and I am in constant contact with other world leaders. It has been decided to issue an outright travel ban. This means that as of 0.800 hours no planes or boats will be coming in or going out. We are also suspending public transport until such time that it is deemed safe to resume. Please keep yourselves up to date with progress. Visit the CDC website for regular updates. If anyone wants to offer their time and services, please go to your local police station where you will be advised on how to proceed. At present we are no wiser as to what caused this outbreak or as to how the virus originated. We do know that the virus attacks the body and shows similarities to many flu strains. At present, that is all the information we have. Please follow instructions carefully. Your cooperation is needed at this time. My thoughts and prayers go out to anyone affected by this.

I repeat, your co-operation is needed at this time. Please pay close attention and follow the instructions of the authorities."

<Guest53>: An interesting read.

<Guest4>: Who wrote that was it you guest5? It was pretty bad, doesn't sound like the Presidents usual speeches I can't find the video of it and I would have expected him to personally address us all on TV to reassure us! If it is right by him or at least meant to be then he is long gone! Probably on the fucking moon by now!!

<Guest39>: Yes and you can guess where he will be, tucked up in bed drinking hot chocolate and eating caviar whilst he is surrounded by armed guards in a luxury underground condo! The chances of the president contracting this are the same as the chances of me dating a supermodel!

<Guest30>: I'm so scared; we are all being moved away from the city…

<Guest31>: @Guest5 not very reassuring is it or helpful but exactly what I would have expected! You can only destroy them, once they have turned, by destroying the brain itself, unless the brain is damaged enough or destroyed they will keep omen trying to infect you and eat your flesh.

<Guest71>: Worries over mystery flu virus as the first cases of this virus have been reported in the U.S, it appears they may have been infected whilst travelling in Cairo or Mexico "Pretty Vague or what?". Comes in from an official news source! C-5…

<Guest31>: It seems like they are trying to infect everyone. Like the virus itself is clever and it knows that biting and spreading the virus is part of its plan in some way, making it stronger.

<Guest4>:This is certainly one way to stop overpopulation, watched a documentary last year saying in the year 219 we would be overpopulated, this was made by the government, I bet they're all safe now while we rot and burn .

<Guest53>: Watching the news and there are reports the president will be giving an official live interview, probably the one from the text above with an actor playing the president CGI anyone!, a bit of a coincidence the president had a busy week planned this week with state visits don't you think?

<Guest32>: Get hold of some oxygen, I've been told that oxygen can kill most germ and even some form of cancer, my grandson's ill and we found this out from a newspaper article.

<Guest33>: I pissed my pants!

<Guest33>: These mindless diseased corpses will stop at nothing to devour your flesh.

I don't know why but the virus makes them have this constant hunger until the brain is destroyed, then your flesh is fair game to them.

<Guest29>: Who would actually want to survive this anyway?

<Guest39>: I just shat myself, I think I went one better than you!!!!!!!!

<Guest33>: I am so confused, we are getting no concrete answers here so standard influenza most commonly spreads through the air normally from a direct act of sneezing or coughing, so let me get this right you can catch this virus from coming into direct contact with someone infected and from the video's we have seen online it will show all the symptoms mentioned in the flu into leaflet then it will kill you and bring you back as a rabid blood thirsty being taking over the brain itself!

But if you are lucky enough not to catch this flu directly you can catch it by one of the infected biting you. So basically the virus is airborne and can also be transmitted by blood. I'm confused no one is either denying or confirming anything.

<Guest43>: my husband came down with flu yesterday. He was bringing up blood in his mucus when he coughed. He was a chain smoker so I put it down to that. He didn't stop coughing a wheezing all day. He's gone now, The Virus took him, he died in hospital, and I am all alone.

<Guest19>: me @guest29! I want to survive this! The world has gone to shit, why are you all on here chatting? It's just plain sad!

<Guest66>: Shops for food, drink and first aid are no longer an option, I have seen big chain stores on fire every shop here has been looted and all that is left is a shell and broken glass.

<Guest50>: There are so many mystery diseases that doctors here in the United Kingdom can't even put a name too, I saw my Doctor look on a bloody search engine in front of me, looking up the symptoms, my wife came back from helping out in a mission in a third world country a good few years ago, we were Ill for weeks and weeks and to be honest I've never felt a hundred percent since contracting the virus. We both had a high fever similar symptoms to swine flu, we thought it was that but the cough was the worst part it lasted for months even with treatment!

We still don't really know what it was it was diagnosed as a severe case of Influenza by a very confused Doctor who had to put a name to the virus!

<Guest59>: Just seen an article online that American citizens are having their guns confiscated by the army even if you have a legal gun license the guns are being taken off of you! I assume if there is any truth to this story that they need back up weapons and ammo for the situation or that they may be able to control crowds better if angry and pissed people don't have guns!

<Guest67>: The standard influenza virus is known to peak on day 2 if this is day 1 what the hell will day 2 be like?

<Guest42>: I'm shaking violently and can't keep anything down, what should I do? I'm so scared in case I have it!

<Guest31>: I think you just got to wait it out, it shouldn't be long now with symptoms like that.

<Guest67>: This is really scary, my daughter came home from school yesterday with a headache and is showing signs of a standard cold after some research online it says that children are so much more infectious with the flu virus than adults and they

shed the virus even before they actually develop symptoms.

<Guest61>: It's OK you will all be fine as none of you have any brains at all!

<Guest31>: There are rumours that water from the tap is not for safe and people are saying to only drink bottled water. No one really knows the cause and everyone is taking every precaution.

<Guest37>: knock knock! Who's there? A million bastard zombies knocking at the door (Just thought I'd lighten the mood a little).

<Guest49>: I can't see out of my windows for the smoke but I can just hear piercing screams and sirens.

<Guest37>: My weed-Whacker is at the ready, I've got a hammer and a baseball bat! I'm going to take out as many as I can! Before I get eaten alive!

<Guest56>: We're all doomed.

<Guest62>: So we are facing more than one threat it looks that way so basically we are all screwed. The odds of staying safe against the virus/the infected and millions of people rioting and looting with no laws in place are slim.

There are videos online of people in the Middle East being stripped down and sprayed with some kind of disinfectant chemical, these people don't even look infected!

If this virus is airborne we are done for…a single sneeze can release as much as 40,000 droplets!

<Guest56>: That is all fucked up and really scary!!

Could this be related to the recent Ebola pandemic?

<Guest69>: There were reports of successful cases of cures for ebola using blood plasma, Have they tried that for this virus! Using blood plasma?

<Guest31>: @Guest56 – To tell you the truth, I don't think so. The incubation rate would have to change considerably, and the last time I looked Ebola wasn't airborne. But that is interesting about blood plasma, and if that was successful for Ebola, then I assume it will at least be considered…

<Guest13>: You are a bunch of arseholes, stop chatting you dicks!

<Guest63>: Infrastructure has been broken down and this happened so quickly which is fucking scary. Surely they were expecting this as they have sent out the info about a flu pandemic.

<Guest67>: Help me please! I'm worried sick here and all alone.

<Guest37>: "Chernobyl" Is this next? The second Chernobyl on a larger scale would it not be easier to wipe everyone out or at least the countries infected at this time so we can all be safe like Chernobyl this surely was a big chain of fuckups and mistakes made my man.. Or a woman! Can't be sexist!

<Guest16>: The shit is hitting the fan, anyone got any ideas?

<Guest43>: Once bitten they seem to jolt into a fast zombie-like state which lasts for around 2/3 minutes then they begin to slow down.

<Guest53>: This is it, it's happening, I've locked my doors, no police, army or walking dead are getting in or my me and family out.

<Guest39>: Help Me Please

<Guest43>: We all need help now, but there is no help here!

<Guest37>: I can hear them at the door!

<Guest37>: Help us...

<Guest58>: I wish I could.

No Data Received
Cannot load page/Error/Error234

Found documented phone recording from the archive.

October 10th 2019

Ron: "Are you there, Kate?

"Ring me as soon as you get this sweetheart. I'm at the army barracks. There's been some kind of a situation. Nobody seems to be sure what's actually going on but it looks like it's got all the signs of a terrorist attack.

"The army and police came knocking door to door this morning just before I was about to leave for work. You must have missed them by about forty minutes. The neighbours are here. The army are gathering civilians and bringing them here, where it's safe. They're keeping us all separate, everyone from our road's in one section. They won't let us leave. They've got armed guards at the doors and...well, I just want to know you're safe. Ring me! I need to know you're OK."

Katie: "Hi, dad!"

Ron: "Thank God...are you OK?"

Katie: "Just about!

"Dad, I'm scared...there was an explosion about ten feet from our bus. We're OK. We waited with the driver by the side of the road but no one came. People were passing us on foot. No one knew what was going on...the traffic came to a standstill, and everyone abandoned their cars."

Ron: "Kate, where are you?"

Katie: "I'm in a field somewhere, with Sarah, John and Caz. We had to break away from the group...something...something happened to them. I know this sounds crazy but they turned, they were manic! Something happened to their eyes. It was like they were suddenly taken over...There was blood everywhere! They started biting people! We ran, Dad. We ran till we didn't see anyone."

Ron: "You need to keep hidden, baby. The army are out there. They'll fix this but you need to stay hidden."

Katie: "We're safe enough for now, but, Dad, it's getting dark."

Ron: "Kate, can you tell me exactly where you are."

Katie: "I don't know...we...we just ran!"

Ron: "Listen to me Kate...on no account do you guys leave each other. You need to find some shelter for the night, before it gets dark. Do you have anything to eat or drink on you?"

Katie: "Not much, just some crisps, chocolate and a couple of cans of drink."

Ron: "Ration it out, Kate. We don't know how long this is going to last."

Katie: "Please don't say that, Dad, that's really not what I need to hear right now."

Ron: "I know, sweetie, I know, but I'll get to you one way or another, don't worry."

Katie: "Please come and get me, Dad, I can't do this on my own, I want you here with me."

Ron: "They're not letting anyone out of here at the moment. They're using force to keep us here and not giving us any information as to what's going on. But it's safe, you need to make your way here. How much battery do you have left on your mobile?"

Katie: "Um… It's nearly fully charged."

Ron: "Good."

Katie: "Dad, I'm so scared! You have to see them…they just started attacking everyone! Their eyes were bloodshot, there was no emotion in their faces. It all happened so quickly, I just didn't know what to do."

Ron: "This is a joke, a bloody bad joke."

Katie: "I wish it was, Dad. I wish it was."

Ron: "Katie, try to find shelter under some trees and stay there tonight. Don't try to move. Tell your friends, your dad knows what he's talking about and he says, stay put for tonight."

Katie: "I'll stay here, Dad. We all will."

Ron: "Someone needs to keep watch. You'll need to take it in shifts."

Katie: "OK, Dad."

Ron: "Make sure you don't attract any attention to yourselves. Keep your voices down and no light or music on your mobiles. It'll be cold through the night – but don't light a fire, and if you see or hear anything untoward move. All of you move, but stay together."

Katie: "OK."

Ron: "Stay safe and make sure that at least one person is on watch at all times."

Katie: "I miss you, Dad. I'll text you in the morning, and you can ring me back. Bye, Dad, I love you."

Ron: "Be careful, darling, and remember what I said…stay safe."

October 11th 2019
07.00 am

Ron: "Kate, are you OK?"

Katie: "Dad, it's so good to hear your voice! We're all fine. We kept watch through the night but it was pretty quiet. We played that movie game, you know, the one that we always play? It kept us awake but Sarah said I must have been cheating, using an app or something, because I won every game."

Ron: "I'm so glad you got through the night OK. I've been so worried. It's crazy here, kind of feels like some 1940's bomb shelter, all huddled together, waiting for the bomb to drop. I really don't know how this situation will progress. No one's giving us any information. I've tried to speak to someone in charge but they won't let me. We think they'll shoot us if we try to leave, so no one's willing to try. I don't have much choice but to stay here, at least for the time being."

Katie: "What the hell do we do now, Dad? We're getting ready to move, but where do we go?"

Ron: "There's no chance of making it back here, it's too much of a risk. You really need to find a safe place to wait it out...what can you see around you?"

Katie: "Nothing apart from the motorway and miles and miles of fields. What do we do, Dad?"

Ron: "Keep away from the roads. Stay together and go quietly and cautiously through the fields."

Katie: "What! Just walk aimlessly through the fields?"

Ron: "You need to find somewhere safe to see it through."

Katie: "We've had most of our food and drink, there's only a can of cola left. Everyone's starving. I could murder one of your famous fry-ups right now, Dad."

Ron: "Me too, honey. We'll be sitting in our kitchen, and I'll be making my famous French toast before you know it. For now, be safe, sweetie. Travel carefully and look out for food and drink wherever you can find it."

Katie: "Speak later, Dad. Love you loads."

Ron: "You'll be fine, honey, love you, bye...bye."

October 11th 2019
17:31pm

Katie: "Dad, Kaz is gone. I'm so so scared!"

Ron: "What do you mean – gone?"

Katie: "She's dead, Dad! We found a farm. It took about three hours to walk there and we didn't see a soul in all that time, except two men walking in the opposite direction, toward the road. But that was just after we set off. When we found the farmhouse, the door had been broken in and Kaz was so excited that we'd found food and shelter. She drank a bottle of whisky that was on the side and ate an apple from the fruit bowl. She was so happy, Dad. She was dancing around the room singing. Then she ran upstairs. We shouted after her, John and I. We told her to wait, but she just kept going. John started to run after her but it was too late.

"We heard her scream, and then she came to the top of the stairs. She was bitten, Dad. Her arm was dripping with blood. She kept screaming as she ran past us on the stairs. Then someone else appeared, he was covered in blood. He had bullet holes in his chest. His eyes were empty. We were all desperately looking around the room for a weapon when John shot him. It forced him down to the floor, but it didn't kill him. He started to get up from the floor and John shot him again – in the head this time, and this time he didn't get up. We dragged his body out of the house and we've tried to secure the doors and windows as best we can. But I'm scared, Dad. I'm really scared."

Ron: "Jesus, are you hurt, Kate?"

Katie: "No, I'm not, just shaken, we all are. This feels like a really bad dream, Dad. I just want to wake up. We sat Kaz down on a chair, gave her some whisky and John poured some over the bite. We found a first aid kit and bandaged her arm up, but she blacked out. John checked for a pulse but there wasn't one. We didn't know what to do, Dad, but then she sat bolt upright and went for John. Dad, it was like it wasn't her anymore! Her eyes were red and she was making a noise like some kind of animal.

"Sarah was shouting and screaming that we needed to get her out of the house. Then there was a loud bang. My ears were ringing and everything seemed to be happening in slow motion. Kaz fell to the ground. There was blood pouring over the stone floor. Sarah was screaming and punching John. I managed to pull her off of him and we just stood there crying."

Ron: "I'm…I'm so sorry you had to go through that, sweetheart. Are the rest of you OK? Kate, remember, you do what you have to do to protect yourself, whatever that may mean."

Katie: "I'm still in shock, Dad. We'd known each other forever, we'd been friends since nursery and now…well…now she's gone. Why is this happening to us, Dad?"

Ron: "I'm sorry, Kate. This is all so wrong! But hold tight, Kate. This will all be over soon and I'll be coming for you. Do you have any food supplies?"

Katie: "Yeah, there's enough food and drink for an army here."

Ron: "OK, that's good, Kate. I know it's the last thing you feel like doing but make sure you all eat something, you need to keep your strength up. Find as many weapons as you can, secure the house and wait it out."

Katie: "We need to secure the place. We had to get Kaz out. We buried her, Dad. We tried to give her a proper send off. We all said a few words and John laid a cross over the ground…Why is this happening? It isn't fair, Dad! Kaz wouldn't hurt a fly, and this is the hand that God dealt her!"

Ron: "Kate, stop talking like that! You need to be strong. You need to board the doors with anything you have. Make sure you can still see out so that someone can keep a lookout at all times. And for God's sake, Kate, don't let anyone in. They could be infected by whatever this is, or take over the farmhouse and leave you stranded in the middle of nowhere again. Just wait it out. Don't move from there, and ration out what food and drink you have. Keep weapons close by and try and keep any light to a minimum, you don't want to attract attention to yourselves.

"It's strange here today. They've separated us into small groups, and it's feeling more and more like we're prisoners of war. We're in groups of ten. I'm with ten men around my age and they're keeping us in a locked room and rationing the food and water. They're still not telling us anything. Everyone just wants to get out of here. There's a window but all we can see is a huge fence and a few military guards patrolling the area."

Katie: "You're safe there though, Dad. Stay put and don't do anything stupid."

Ron: "OK, sweetheart, which goes for you too. We'll talk tomorrow, love you, Kate."

October 12th 2019
07:13am

Katie: "It was quiet last night, Dad. The silence was quite eerie but we slept well and felt a lot safer with the house boarded up. We cooked on the wooden stove this morning. I think we've enough logs to last the year. We just cooked up a few tins and we're having a look around to see what could be useful."

Ron: "I'm glad you're OK. Five of our group were taken today. They didn't say what was happening, they just took them off. Later, I saw a big trolley going past and I caught a glimpse of the jeans that one of our group, bloke called, Tom, was wearing. We think they're killing us off. Maybe there's not enough food, or maybe they were infected, but either way I want out of this hellhole. I feel like a sitting duck. We might have been exposed to something, I mean, who knows?"

Katie: "Dad, you're scaring me! Get out of there! Don't take any chances."

Ron: "I've got to go now, honey. I'll speak to you later, love you."

October 12th 2019
13:05pm

Ron: "Kate, I'm OK."

Kate: "It's so good to hear your voice, I didn't know if you were…"

Ron: "We're out of there, Kate, all five of us! We smashed the window and we got the hell out of there. The fence was covered in barbed wire – we all just went for it at the same time. We were spotted and told to get down or they'd shoot. They started firing. Max and James fell. James didn't get up but Max was just wounded, shot in the arm, until he ran screaming and shouting straight into a guard, hell he had some guts! The guard shot him in the head but the three of us managed to scramble over. We ran like crazy! Pete was behind and he shouted out to let us know that they were opening the gates, coming after us. Two of the guards were chasing us, firing at us. Pete was shot. They just kept shooting and he just kept running. He gave it his all, then hid behind the trees as we went into the forest.

"The guards were calling out – they were saying that they wouldn't shoot if we came out with our hands above our heads. When they'd finished speaking, there was an almighty scream. David and I looked at each other, thinking it was one of us, but as we turned, we saw what looked like a zombie from a horror film, tearing the flesh from one of the guard's legs. They were both shooting at it, they must have fired about ten times at point blank range, till he finally went down. The wounded soldier was on the floor, writhing and screaming, the other dropped his gun.

"Just as we turned to try and creep away, about six zombies appeared from nowhere, heading directly for the wounded guard. The guard reached for his gun and started to fire like crazy, most of the bullets were just hitting the trees. The zombies closed in, and within minutes, both the guards were just a mass of organs and blood. Without thinking, I ran and grabbed for the guns, only, when I picked the second one up, I attracted a zombie's attention and he started to walk toward me. I shot him in the head and he went down instantly, then the others started to walk toward us. I threw David the second gun and within seconds the zombies were dead.

"We ran for what seemed like forever – over fields. There were zombies all over the place, mostly on their own. We didn't want to attract attention, so we didn't fire, we just steered clear of them. We've made a shelter, with branches and twigs, so we should be safe for the night. We've had some berries but I could murder a decent meal."

Katie: "I'm glad you got out of there, Dad. I was worried about you. Can you make it here?"

Ron: "The phone's on one bar, honey. I'll try and get to you, I promise."

Katie: "OK. Night, Dad, love you."

Ron: "You too, speak soon."

October 12th 2019
19:48pm

Ron: "Kate, are you OK? I-I've...run into some trouble. I fell asleep. I woke up and I...I...It was biting my leg! I managed to get away OK, but I'm feeling a bit worse for wear now. It was about three minutes ago, Kate. I had to speak to you, in case...well, you know...in case I turn into one of those...those things! I've tried to stop the bleeding but I'm losing too much, Kate...I'm so sorry, Kate."

Katie: "Dad, what the bloody hell happened? I'm scared shitless!"

Ron: "I love you, darling, always have, always will. I'll be with you forever. Stay strong my little fighter."

Katie: (Crying) "Dad, I love you! You're the best dad and friend anyone could ever wish for. I love you, Dad!"

Ron: "My little ray of sunshine. I love you so much! You're stronger than you know, honey. You've always been my rock. When I thought I'd never smile again, you made me, honey. I love you! Thank you so much!"

Single gunshot.

Katie: "Dad...Dad...Dad!"

Forum archived from the day the pandemic hit across the globe.

Mystery Flu Virus possible epidemic?

PrepperMax
Member
Moderator
October 10th : 2019

I know this is a bit off topic but, I have just been reading a few of the articles online about this mystery flu virus/pandemic.

I thought it worth a post just to see what everyone thinks.

There are reports of a "mystery illness" that has already claimed over fifty lives in Cairo and Benha.

I also read about a case in Mexico!

There are now over a thousand cases of this "mystery virus" the numbers are rising and there are rumours of mass quarantines being put in place. It's worrying knowing that over fifty people have already died from this "mystery virus" in only twenty-four hours, that's what we are being told through the news channels. So God knows what is really going on?

This is freaky; does anyone know anything about it? Do you think this is really worth worrying about, or is it me just being my usual paranoid self?

Prepper Max

#1
Jimsster
Member
October 10th : 2019

I would not worry, I've got some paracetamol in and some aspirin.

Look at all the hype around Swine Flu!

These kinds of things are cropping up all the time. It might be a problem in these third world countries where they do not have proper hand sanitation and access to medicines and proper treatment...
But we would not see a wide spread pandemic in this day and age!

#2
Reece
Member
October 10th : 2019

@Max
To be honest I personally would not worry too much, I know what you are like any hint of anything or a rumour or a whisper your on it like a fly around shit! Don't get me wrong I know you are a real prepper and probably get some kind of buzz from doing it but tell me this if any kind of apocalypse hit would you really be prepared, I think you can discard all the food weapons or supplies for any situation they will become less than useless if you freeze if you are not prepared and put in a fight or flight situation not everyone knows how they will really react when the shit hits the fan! No matter what the cause is, I was worried as hell about swine flu and Ebola but everything is now under control I think people have lack of faith with the government.
If this is the news swine flu etc. It will be contained do you really think all the VIP's will want to get it! No chance there is nothing money can't buy!

Please don't worry yourself Max! This was not meant as malice it is me trying to reassure a very nice person!

I'm off to bed not before a long bath with some muscle soak bloody nightshift kills me!

Have a good one all!

#3
Prepper Max
Member
Moderator
October 10th : 2019

@Reece
I know, buddy, we're pals. No worries. You know me, I'll always do what I feel is right!

For me and everyone! All those who are interested!

Enjoy that soak – let the tension go!!

I have just found this information from looking online:

100 people in Cairo tested positive for H5N1 avian flu in the past month.

Fifty people in China tested positive for H7N9 Avian Influenza virus in the last few months.

In 2013 alone there were over 132 humans infected with H7N9 and well over 44 deaths.

There are reports of the virus turning up in poultry all over.

It must have something to do with this. There are far too many cases like this lately for it not to be connected.

#4
Barbara56
Member
October 10th : 2019

I agree with you Max! I'm interested:

I'm keeping a very close eye on this!

I did hear something on the radio about a flu virus but missed the start of it, then this post caught my eye!

Is this connected in any way to the canine H3N8 or the swine flu outbreak from 2009 H1N1?

#5

Vicky1

Guest

October 10th : 2019

@Barbara56

It may be a mutated strain who knows!

I would not worry too much! I agree with @Reece.

These viruses and so called "new flu's" seem to be cropping up a lot lately. To be honest, I don't read too much into it, I think I would worry myself silly if I did.

#6

Prepper Max

Member

Moderator

October 10th : 2019

On the news a minute ago it said a large number of troops have been deployed to handle the virus in Cairo.

This is crazy!

@Reece next time listen to me!!!

#7
Caitlin
Member
October 10th : 2019

Cases are popping up all over the globe. It does seem to be an epidemic in these foreign countries, with all the commuting it won't be long before we get it over here, I live in New York City. Did scientists create this new deadly flu virus? This is the topic on the radio station I'm listening to now.

It says that a research laboratory in China last year was deliberately engineering new types of hybrid strains of the bird-flu virus and human influenza which, if executed the right or wrong way could cause a pandemic.

Scary to think that this was in the news just a matter of months ago.

#8
Gimleyx
Member
October 10th : 2019

That is scary stuff!

What gives them the right to play God anyway? It's bullshit.

There should at least be the correct containment protocols in place. I'm sure that there are many countries, all over the globe, that have deadly viruses but they would never let them escape. Just imagine the clearance needed to get in somewhere like that. I always think of these weird scenarios like: one day a man finds out that his wife has cancer and goes crazy – thinks life's not fair and releases a deadly virus by giving it to himself, then getting on a plane or something – as easy as that.

#9
Kendo19
Member
October 10th : 2019

Surely that's life? You don't moan at them when they discover breakthrough cures. The risk is worth it to produce the break-throughs in medical science.

#10
Prepper Max
Member
Moderator
October 10th : 2019

very similar to this. It looks like this could be a super virus. That will get mass media attention. But I study this kind of thing, I know I'm sad, but while most people watch TV soaps or read a sexy book, I'm looking at patterns – no, not knitting patterns! Even down to things in the press and the media; how and what info they give away to people. If it's something that could be a worldwide epidemic, like the measles a few years ago, they nicely say, I think everyone should get their child vaccinated – they announce it globally. Well, at least in the countries that can afford it! As you mention, "swine flu" seems outbreak. UK and US residents received a leaflet with guidelines telling people the best ways to avoid contracting the flu virus. "Wash your hands" bin it, was another big campaign – if you use a tissue – bin it. This is far worse! I can see that the reports are already coming in much faster from reliable sources: radio, TV, online!

This is going to be big guys and girls!

Trust me!

Start preparing now!

#11

Caitlin

Member

October 10th : 2019

There is footage all over the internet of people attacking, biting and even attempting to eat one another. It is rumoured to be from Cambodia it does look like it is there from the scenery.

Is this connected to the virus?

#12

Mick22

Member

October 10th : 2019

There's nothing on the news channels yet just a bunch of videos and stories all over the internet. There are far too many accounts for this not to be really happening, this is either the best hoax in the world or the end of it.

Either way it's pretty messed up!

#13

JamesTK

Member

October 10th : 2019

You guys are right there are so many websites covering this!

Did none of you hear the news last night, may be due to the time change, here in the London England there was a report of a mystery flu virus.

#14
Reece
Member
October 10th : 2019

You will laugh at this not a lot! But I'm in the bath with some classic rock a bear and a smoke unwinding! And what the fuck comes on the radio in a news bulletin;
"Worries over mystery flu virus as first cases of the virus have been reported in the us It does seem as if the patients contracted the virus whilst travelling in Cairo other passengers have been informed and are or will be quarantined."
I know this is some online rock radio station but there will be some credibility to the @Max need I say anything else!

#15
Prepper Max
Member
Moderator
October 10th : 2019

This is unreal!
Medical teams are rumoured to be in Garden City Cairo. There are even reports that the town is now completely under quarantine.
It's rumoured to be total mayhem down there.
Google Maps Shows a Mystery Flu Virus, "Public Alerts" and Warnings.

Keep track to see if it has hit your area/state/country yet!

Latest headlines!

This is one report from an online UK news site.

First deadly case of this flu reported in the UK.

Widespread panic: people are stockpiling.

If you are forced to leave cities, or heavily populated towns, carry enough food and water, a weapon and a first aid kit with you. Wear clothing such as leather and pad all of your clothing out to avoid it being bitten through and the skin being pierced. Cardboard and duct tape can come in very handy.

If you are setting out on the road you will run out of food pretty quickly. Don't chance going in a car and avoid attracting attention if you are going out there. Remember you can eat certain plants and berries. Spend a short time learning what plants and berries are safe to eat. Grab sugar and take it on the road with you, also things like bananas are great for slow release energy. Avoid supermarkets and other stores as looting and fighting has broken out.

A good drink to carry with you on the go is a bottle of water with half a teaspoon of sugar and half a teaspoon of salt.

#16
JamesTK
Member
October 10th : 2019

The news says it is a virus that may be causing strange side effects in the young, those with immune deficiencies or anyone not strong enough to handle the virus. There is a guy on there now saying the videos are hoaxes but this virus is real.

Pretty worried here, there is a much higher police presence than usual!

#17
Lennon
Guest
October 10th : 2019

I think this is more likely to have something to do with MERS (Middle Eastern Respiratory Syndrome) virus.

In 2012 the virus was first reported and named MERS as sufferers were from around the Arabian peninsula. In 2014 there was global panic as cases were reported in France, UK, U.S, China and Russia. The virus is spread through close contact and the symptoms consist of:

Severe acute respiratory illness
Fever
Cough
Shortness of breath

There are rumors online of similar symptoms being reported. The scary thing is that as it's a respiratory disease it can spread very easily and very fast!
Around 60% of people infected with the virus will die!

#18
Maxxyboy
Guest
October 10th : 2019

Coronavirus (MERS) has been present for over 15 years in camels.
The virus itself is very similar to the SARS virus, though

rumoured not to spread that easily. As with most flu's and respiratory virus's people with underlying health issues and weak immune systems are most at risk.

#19
Jackson55
Member
October 10th : 2019

What kind of alternative medicine can be taken at home to prevent us getting this flu?
Obviously we can't all get to the doctors to get a vaccine for MERS or cattle flu (if one even exists). Please help, I'm worried because I have chest problems anyway,
Thanks.

#20
AlexEvans
Guest
October 10th : 2019

I would start taking raw garlic and lots of it! The allicin in the garlic will be released when garlic is crushed and chopped, its best eaten about 10 minutes after being chopped. Garlic is a natural antibiotic even the Romans used it. Get as much garlic down you as you can, there have even been reports that it can cure cancer!
Look it up!

#21
Wrestleking
Guest
October 10th : 2019

I would recommend using colloidal silver, which consists pretty much of silver particles suspended in liquid. Colloidal silver can be used to treat colds, sore throats, infections, un-sanitized water and can also be used in place of antibiotics. You swallow the liquid or use on open cuts or sores. The UK alone spent £25 million on dressings containing silver for patients. This stuff is fantastic; it used to be used in place of antibiotics.

I take a variety of things if I think I'm getting a cold/flu CS/ACV and Garlic.

#22
EwanSam
Guest
October 10th : 2019

I would try honey and cinnamon (in a dry form). Put a teaspoon of cinnamon in a cup of hot water with 2 teaspoons of honey, this is a known cure for a cold or flu and will reduce symptoms significantly.

Another good one is apple cider vinegar, a teaspoon taken in cold water is ideal, I even gargle daily with it, spend some time and look them up online, and these are the best home remedies out there to my knowledge.

#23
Jackson55
Member
October 10th : 2019

Thank you so much for the tips, I have heard of ACV but not heard or tried the silver, that sounds interesting or honey and cinnamon together, I'm quite a fan of cinnamon, so I'll try some of that today.

#24
Chipper89
Guest
October 10th : 2019

Damn I love that Honey and Cinnamon, my granny used to swear by it!
I use a teaspoon of manuka honey daily; it wards off any kind of cold or flu.
There are a few reports of the virus but it really won't be that bad, try not to worry yourselves sick!

#25
BrentChilds
Member
October 10th : 2019

Get yourself at least 2500mg of vitamin C, the ascorbic acid neat vitamin C is best (without that evil sorbitol in it)
Or you may be on the toilet all day!

Nothing happening or occurring yet here in Barcelona.
I now fancy honey and cinnamon @ Jackson/Chipper
But I would have a large whiskey in mine!

#26
Razor44
Member
October 10th : 2019

My mum used to swear by keeping a cut up onion in a saucer in every room of the house If she thought we were coming down with a cold, don't ask me why but it always worked.
She also made us eat a clove of raw garlic a day!

#27
Jackson55
Guest
October 10th : 2019

Thanks for all the tips!
It's worth a try to boost immunity to the flu virus;
Just realized it may not be as easy to get out my street has been blocked of barricaded either end we have been told to stay indoors!
So it's a big cupboard raid here!

#28
Aaron31
Guest
October 10th : 2019

You are all arseholes!

Police block my arse this guy is bull shiting!

Here in Scotland there is not even a whisper of anything like that ok so flu is in a different country .

Calm down all, there is nothing to worry about. If you are that worried stay indoors, but I won't be staying in.

Get over it. I'm off to the pub, to watch the football.

Come on you Reds!

But before that porn sites here I come!

#29
JamesTK
Member
October 10th : 2019

You wanker!

No trust me it is real!

All it says on the news is that a flu-like virus has been reported in the countries mentioned and that there have been fatalities.

 # 30
Vicky1
Guest
October 10th : 2019

I've Just been ushered out from a play in central New York, apparently one of the actors was sick and it was a health risk. We were pushed out like cattle and when we left the theatre I could hear screaming. I'm on my way home now; I can see the queue at the station from here. There are sirens and a large police presence all over.

Is this related to Ebola?

What is Ebola mutated with a super flu?
Would this be it!

#31
Caitlin
Member
October 10th : 2019

No, they would know if it was Ebola and they would tell us for sure. It could be a mutation of the flu virus who knows? Viruses do mutate and grow stronger, it was rumoured years ago that it was not likely to be the last we were going to see of Swine flu.

#32
Pete
Member
October 10th : 2019

There are well over three thousand suspected cases of the flu virus now and there are reports of over 500 deaths from it. The news channels are going crazy, even the reporters look puzzled. There are reports of attacks, murders and riots all over.
This is far worse than swine flu.
I think we are on the same levels of threat as for the recent Ebola outbreak.
Not being nasty but this is real!
I don't like how one minute everything was fine now, I'm hearing about from many interent radio stations there is a stronger online presence and media around this than on terrestrial TV.

#33
Reece
Member
October 10th : 2019

Where are you getting your figures from?
The figures on the news are a lot lower indeed.

#34
Vicky1
Guest
October 10th : 2019

I had swine flu last year; I was so ill and nearly died. I was put on antibiotics and even steroids but I pulled through.
The thing is I thought swine flu had vanished I was even admitted to hospital with it for a night!
There are a lot of things they don't like to put in the news and to cause a worldwide panic could me much worse!
This sounds a lot worse than swine flu; I never had blood from my chest or nose with swine flu.

#35
Jason23x
Guest
October 10th : 2019

It's saying on some of the internet news sites that it's now a Flu Epidemic.
If it is don't be too worried!

Just type a random word or disease on the internet and you will pull up hundreds if not thousands of results ... That's why you are seeing more online because you are looking for it and that's why there is not much on the main worldwide news!

I hate people you have nothing better to do than just read bullshit and panic.

#36
Caitlin
Member
October 10th : 2019

How can this really be a flu Epidemic?

No one here has the Flu, we usually get flu every year but this year we're are all fine.

The only virus I know going around every year without fail is the Norovirus which causes gastroenteritis.

The one where the house becomones a scene from " The Exorcist" with vomit!

I don't think this is a flu Epidemic yet!.

#37
Walter w
Guest
October 10th : 2019

Apocalypse Now!

"Fucked" we are all Fucked!

Get of the internet and actually try to survive, Having the latest smartphone or tablet is no use too anyone now!

Who are you going to impress "The Dead".

Trust me the internet and phones will all be gone in a matter of hours!

Knowing my luck I will see "Sefies of the Dead" or a new trend on social media for as lomg as it lasts photo bombing with a corpse!

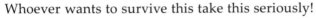

#38
Prepper Max
Member
Moderator
October 10th : 2019

Whoever wants to survive this take this seriously!

You need to gather food, batteries, torches, candles; water and weaponry of any kind.

"ACT NOW"

They're saying that all strains of flu have the ability to cause side effects; this is more dangerous in children, the elderly and those with underlying illnesses.

The news broadcast says they are worried about meningitis and encephalopathy (basically brain disease), as a side effect from this flu. They are reporting that the swelling could cause major changes in perception and other neurological symptoms to show up.

Start prepping now – You will need a long term survival plan, not just for a day or two!

If this does reach peak!

#39
JamesTK
Member
October 10th : 2019

That's worrying stuff Max.

Holy shit!

Have you seen the video that's going round?

I just got it emailed to me, it looks like a rabid man/ zombie eating away at a man until he's just a pile of matter, well until the attacker gets shot. It looks too freakin real to be a fake, the video is reported to originate from Tunisia.

What do you guys think?

This is all freaking me out.

#40
Prepper Max
Member
October 10th : 2019

Yes I have seen the video, it does look real. There are reports of attacks and riots and these seem to be coming from Tunisia, Mexico, Benha and Cairo. These are all places where it's hot and humid and people come into close contact with animals. It's basically a breeding ground for a mutated virus. Are they connected or is this one big coincidence. ??

#41
Bertiexx
Member
October 10th : 2019

The first thing to look at is how credible the sources of the videos are.

Where did the information come from?

I do not believe anything yet I, not going to start packing just yet or shitting my pants. All I know is that yes there are riots and attacks in these areas but is it just because the lime light is on these areas with the hype and media surrounding the flu???? Do they have these troubles normally in these countries? Yes they do, they are always rioting and shooting one another.

Food for thought.

#42
Gez
Member
October 10th : 2019

I'm in Wales,

I can only find reports online, this is the third page like this I've come across whilst filtering through the conspiracy theory websites (they're always fun to read). Something big must be going on, there are videos that look so real online of rabid attacks, I hope this is a hoax, if it is it's the best one yet and it's not even April 1st or Halloween.

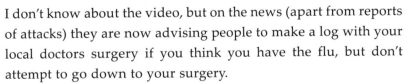

#43
Stanley
Member
October 10th : 2019

I don't know about the video, but on the news (apart from reports of attacks) they are now advising people to make a log with your local doctors surgery if you think you have the flu, but don't attempt to go down to your surgery.

(Which tells us something big is going down!)

They are also saying...

Make sure that you wash your hands frequently, don't touch your mouth, nose or even your eyes and use alcohol based hand washes.

Don't go out if you think you have it (if possible). Cough or sneeze into your elbow or facing to the floor, and throw away used tissues quickly.

#44
Caitlin
Member
October 10th : 2019

What are they calling this virus?

#45
Ziggy45
Member
October 10th : 2019

People are calling it cow flu/cattle flu or at least stating on some sites this may be the origin!
I don't know! I don't think it is as basic as mutated cattle flu or even Ebola.

#46
Caitlin
Member
October 10th : 2019

Really– cow flu!
Quite unoriginal, the name alone doesn't sound that menacing (though mad cow disease was never fun).
At least it didn't claim that many victims and I still enjoy a nice burger now and then. It's got to have lots of cheese in it, relish

and ketchup or burger sauce!
Though I have been told I am a bit mad.
JK I'll STFU now.

47
Karyn17
Guest
October 10th : 2019

I know that (H1N1) is a virus from duck origin and that they have
used the name (H3N2) for a virus from a human origin.

#48
Reece
Member
October 10th : 2019

I thought (H1N1) was swine flu?

#49
Prepper Max
Member
Moderator
October 10th : 2019

Yes H1N1 is swine flu. It may have started from a duck origin
who knows?
I do like duck and orange, I could have that and some sticky rice
about now.

#50
Stanley
Member
October 10th : 2019

@Ziggy45
"People are calling it cow flu?"
I think the correct term is Cattle flu, which is what they are calling it at the moment, well on the news channel I am watching now anyway. They are saying it may be Cattle Flu and there are lots of people mentioning (MERS) - Coronavirus too.

#51
Bill69
Member
October 10th : 2019

Just came across this site, I'm in Australia and the news network has been inundated with reports that there maybe a terrorist attack, or that one is imminent. There are reports of a virus spreading. This is all I know at the moment though it seems really quiet around this area at the moment.

#52
Erina
Member
October 10th : 2019

I'm so scared, I have heard reports from all over the internet of a virus that is causing people to have flu like symptoms and cough up blood, there are also reports of cannibalistic attacks from all over the country.

They have got to be connected it's so terrifying. We are all staying inside, though we did manage to get to the store for some supplies.

It was like Christmas eve in there though (good job we weren't after tinned ham).

#53
Prepper Max
Member
Moderator
October 10th : 2019

Please only give true facts. Don't mislead anyone, you may put someone else in danger or even cause fatalities by giving false information.

I know it's the internet and ninety-nine percent of the stuff online is all bullshit, but this is here to help one another. Please feel free to leave messages for loved ones and friends and keep us posted of anything you find. I will do the same.

I wish everyone luck, stay safe out there. I hope to keep everyone updated with any new info I find.

#54
Mayo
Guest
October 10th : 2019

I've just been sent a clip of a man attacking another man. He bites a chunk from the man's arm and his shoulder, the other man fainted instantly, it's online, people are screaming all around and then the phone gets dropped but you can still hear all the screams.

There is some really weird shit going on here.

#55
Blazer1
Guest
October 10th : 2019

Oh yeah, Photoshop or some new-fangled editor in play I think. Do you really think the government would allow us to even see this shit? They would cover everything up, think Roswell bitches!

You think those videos of Zombie like beings are real?

This has to be bullshit! I believe it is a flu with bad side effects and a global panic! With Chinese whispers!

I like "Night of the Living Dead" as much as the next guy! But Really?

Come the fuck on!!!

#56
Elvira
Guest
October 10th : 2019

I can't get in contact with my family in Spain, I've tried the neighbors but I'm getting really worried now. None of us are showing any signs of infection yet so I think we're ok, but we need more information.

#57
WalkingCadaver
Guest
October 10th : 2019

Who knows what caused this?
For all we know we could have been digesting it all along just like Mad Cow Disease. Especially as this is rumored to be originated from Cattle!!

#58
Orchid33
Member
October 10th : 2019

This is happening, and for it to be happening this fast it can only mean one thing, no one has control over the situation.
We're stocking up on meds, it chaos here in our local supermarket, people are grabbing items out of people's hands and trading items already!!
More and more people are going outside because they need food, drink and weapons——even though we have been told to stay in to reduce chances of spreading the infection.

#59
Olivia19
Member
October 10th : 2019

Please tell me all this is a hoax, I'm worried sick!

If it really is happening then what next?

#60
Zippy
Guest
October 10th : 2019

I've just had a message from my girlfriend saying there are reports that they are evacuating parts of the city of London. She is saying, they are being forced to leave the city and was escorted out, she's safe and there is a large military and police presence there.

#61
Zombie Hunter
Member
October 10th : 2019

There are reports from numerous terror groups claiming that they are responsible for this attack/infection. Reports of over ten different individuals and organisations (well if it is true nine of them are lying are they lying). Does this boost their profile in some way? They do say that there's no such thing as bad publicity.

 # 62
ArmySteve
Member
October 10th : 2019

This is all a bit too real!
I assume it's to do with this mystery Flu virus.

I've had an email from a close friend who works in the media telling me to get out of the city ASAP, it's not be safe here and so on. He wouldn't have sent this unless he was sure, he told me that there have been sightings of military escorts all over London and the United States of America. They are escorting people out I assume VIP's or important people, he didn't say general people- us common folk don't get escorted in stretch limos.

#63
JamesTK
Member
October 10th : 2019

There are many reports of cannibalistic and zombie likes attacks now.
This is really happening!

#64
Zombieking
Guest
October 10th : 2019

Isaiah 26:19
"Thy dead men shall live; together with my dead body shall they arise. Awake and sing, ye that dwell in the dust: for thy dew is as the dew of herbs, and the earth shall cast out the dead."

#65
Prepper Max
Member
Moderator

October 10th : 2019

The numbers are rising by the minute one says suspected 21000 cases and now 2678 deaths, those figures are very worrying, mainly the death toll. I would not take much notice of the suspected figure as when people hear about a virus they instantly think they have it! Even the transport services have been forced to a halt and on the news it said any planes with passengers coming into the UK or the US will be put into immediate quarantine.

It's really scary, it's just swine flu again really but I don't think anyone is willing to take chances. There have been the usual warnings for the elderly, children and anyone with asthma or underlying health issues that will have a high risk factor. Oh and pregnant women, that narrows it down then!

That's a large majority of the population.

It does seem to be causing rabid side effects just like zombies!

The Top Ten places to go in order to survive this type of Crisis/Virus...

Cheyenne Mountain Complex US
Maun sell Sea Forts UK
Missile Silo Homes in the US
Alcatraz Island US
Off Shore Drilling Stations
The Caledon Hatch Nuclear Bunker UK
Aria Towers Brazil
Prisons
Oil Rigs
Survival underground Condos

#66
Barbara56
Member
October 10th : 2019

There are so many reports of what seem to be cannibalistic attacks (zombies) all over the internet, this is fucking insane!
We are not going out of the door, my wife received some mail today and wouldn't even touch it without latex gloves on (apparently the virus can live for a awhile) this is messed up, I'm getting more worried by the minute.

#67
Killer
Member
October 10th : 2019

The Dead Are Walking,

The Dead Are Rising!

It's Official.

#68
Stanley
Member
October 10th : 2019

There are more and more videos up online, it does look like the people attacking are rabid. Whether or not it's from the cattle flu virus I can't say.

#69
James TK
Member
October 10th : 2019

There are reports online that bodies of the victims of the flu decompose instantly after death.
This sounds messed up, it can't be true.

#70
Reece
Member
October 10th : 2019

No @James TK I don't believe that it's not a vampire pandemic…
I've heard the complete opposite, there's a video online of a lady who was bitten and within a few minutes she had a high fever, died and came back with the same symptoms basically like a zombie.

#71
Romero
Guest
October 10th : 2019

They really do look like Zombies! Don't they?
If this is the Zombie Apocalypse!
"It is time to fight back!"

#72
Stanley
Member
October 10th : 2019

There are reports of riots and attacks in Israel, Jordon, Syria, Lebanon and even Kazakhstan there's footage online in Kazakhstan of a mass quarantine in place.

Hold up! More reports coming in on the news of riots in France and now the UK.

There are even videos of what look like hundreds of people fully clothed running screaming and have been burnt alive on fire from the middle east.

Is this how they try to control the virus there…

#73
Tom Vas
Guest
October 10th : 2019

It is spreading, there are no official figures being given out at present here in Moscow.

I watched the News as China, Russia, Australia, Sweden, France, America then the United Kingdom, Australia, Mexico and India just went red, which means infected cases that's when I panicked. The whole world has basically been hit in a matter of hours what the fuck!

Staying in here and going to defend my home from any threat, anyone who comes in dies!

#74
Carlito
Member
October 10th : 2019

One thing's for sure, this is not just your run of the mill seasonal influenza, this is serious.

Whatever it is, matters not!

It's how we deal with the situation at hand, and it doesn't look hopeful!

They need to work from the bottom, find the cause and then stop this spreading!

#75
James TK
Member
October 10th : 2019

There are reports of fatalities from the virus in UK, US, Ireland, Scotland, Wales, France, Spain and now Russia. Apparently a plane was seized when mayhem occurred, someone reported a rabid violent attack.

It looks to me as if the Virus originated in

Mexico or The Middle east and people have flown to the UK and it is spreading outwards from here. I could be wrong though, imagine the stops on flights in Thailand for every person who comes in to contact with just ne of those passengers we are talking about thousands of potential cases, to be honest this is frightening as hell!

#76
Prepper Max
Member
Moderator
October 10th : 2019

Cases/deaths now reported in India, Mongolia, Mexico China, North and South Korea and even Japan. It seems to be spreading at such an uncontrollable rate.

#77
End Game
Member
October 10th : 2019

People laugh and joke but I knew the end was coming soon, it's our punishment for the way we've treated this planet.
I could see this happening, this is our punishment!

#78
Sachi19
Member
October 10th : 2019

This is real, we are in Japan, I have witnessed a man being attacked in the street, he was biting and chewing a man's shoulder like it was a rib of beef. I wasn't close enough to see the end result, I did not see if he turned himself like the rumor's say, but I did not want to hang around, but its mayhem here, we're being told to stay inside on lock down.

79
JamesTK
Member
October 10th : 2019

It is literally causing zombie-like effects. I can't stop watching the videos online I'm shaking while watching them.
This can't really be happening!
Is this a bad dream??

#80
Jakey
Member
October 10th : 2019

Yes James it is really Happening, what do we do now for the best? I'm in the US Here!

#81
Reece
Member
October 10th : 2019

I would head away from the cities and protect yourself as best as you can. Get a weapon and stay away from people.
I know that's what I'm doing.

#82
Prepper Max
Member
Moderator
October 10th : 2019

What a coincidence (or not) the CDC website is rumoured to have been hacked. It was just on the news. I don't think it was hacked, I think the site would have been in meltdown. The clicks that site must have been getting, it would have been more that Twitter and Facebook.

#83
Reece
Member
October 10th : 2019

How weird is that? I've just been on there and it says due to reasons out of our control the site is temporally unavailable. I wouldn't bother checking back there anytime soon, nobody has answers about anything. I turned the news on a minute ago, it was showing pictures of the royal family and what clothes they are wearing????
That's about right.

#84
Matthew12
Guest
October 10th : 2019

Reports now from Thailand, Cambodia and Vietnam, they all now have cases and fatalities from the virus.

"It's causing the patients to go rabid."

There are now reports saying that corpses are coming to life– could this really be true?

#85
Dazza456
Guest
October 10th : 2019

Who knows anything is possible now this shit is happening I wouldn't blink an eye lid if I saw a flying pig today.

Is there a pattern to this or are random people turning rabid/crazy/zombie, and at what stage with the virus?

#86
Stanley
Member
October 10th : 2019

@Dazza456

It seems if you have the virus you will go crazy or rabid. There are reports that if you get bitten/infected you will at first show symptoms of the flu virus then die and come back to life and you will turn rabid.

Jesus, this thing does not mess about does it!!!!

There are reports all over the internet of Flu/deaths and even terror/cannibalistic attacks, appearing in countries all over.

#87
Retroguy
Guest
October 10th : 2019

Reports and deaths now from Nashville, New Mexico, Minnesota, Salem, California and even Maine this thing is everywhere it has swept across the United States so quickly! , basically everywhere, its hit globally nowhere is safe!! This is just what's on the news now.

The Blind are leading the blind only the blind are now the undead!

#88
BattyB
Member
October 10th : 2019

More deaths from Brazil, Argentina Australia and New Zealand It's freaky!

There's a map on the main news channel, every time I look at it somewhere else has turned red, meaning there are reported cases of the virus and deaths in that area.

It seems wherever the virus is reported there are these unexplained cannibal/ rabid attacks.

This really is not a coincidental. It seems the virus causes you to act in this way.

#89
Get off The Internet
Member
October 10th : 2019

"All joking aside why are you guys still on the internet? "
The world is going crazy and you lot are just sitting there, you're all messed up!
Maybe for once you can't defend yourself with words from behind the safety of your computer screen and keyboard.
You are all fucking retarded!
You bunch of fucking Walking Dead's! I will survive you will all fucking die!

#90
Prepper Max
Member
Moderator
October 10th : 2019

STFU, and die!
I'm here to find out as much information as I can and provide all the information that I know. Going by the users who are just viewing this thread alone, I know I'm not the only one. I am being helpful and actually feel I am helping by letting others know any news that I hear and reports of where the flu /virus has struck.
Suspected cases 49467
Deaths 15789
I don't know if this information is factual or not!

#91
Bill23
Guest
October 10th : 2019

You're All Going to die!
Any chance of donating cash to me send all belonging's and cash to me because I will survive I will be the New King of the new world you silly fuckers!
Also is you have a donor card I would throw it away you will all be donating your organs to the zombies as the latest taka way food craze!
The Zombies are here!
They're coming to get you Prepper Max!

#92
Reece
Member
October 10th : 2019

@Bill23
If we die, you dieBill23 so it's not all bad eh.
I'll send something to you! That's for sure! When you get eaten can you get someone to film it and upload it for us!
We all would love to watch that!

#93
Bill23
Guest
October 10th : 2019

Post Deleted.

#94
Prepper Max
Member
Moderator
October 10th : 2019

Bring it on!
Can someone moderate these arseholes please, as I am trying to provide a service here?
The CDC website is down we need somewhere like this.
Please feel free to provide the latest information or news that you hear.

 # 95
Stanley
Member
October 10th : 2019

How long will the internet be up for if it does really go to shit?
I can't see it being long!
A day at best! Maybe more?

#96
Prepper Max
Member
Moderator
October 10th : 2019

To be honest I think we will all die from the virus, the causes or starvation/thirst or killed by looters. Before the internet goes off there's not a man cranking a handle anymore, he stopped a while back. It's done by minions now, all technology now.

97
Stanley
Member
October 10th : 2019

Reports now from Alaska, Argentina, Denmark, Sudan, Africa, Germany, Rome and the Ukraine and Romania. It's a war zone in some areas, there is even footage of trouble at the JFK airport, helicopters and police and a lot of blood, there's rioting and looting everywhere.

#98
Jet234
Guest
October 10th : 2019

I'm in Canada and yes there are reports here now. The whole town has gone crazy, everyone's stockpiling like mad, and you can here gunshots and sirens everywhere.
I'm not scared but if I didn't have this mother of a gun I think I would be. I'm lying, I'm scared of getting the virus but not of any of these attackers or even the looters.
If they try it on me they will really wish that they hadn't.
It's like world war three out there.

#99
AmyQ
Member
October 10th : 2019

This is really scaring me, social media sites are in melt down at the moment, the most popular tags are as follows!
#HealthWarning
#Help
#HelpUs
#HelpMe
#PleaseHelp
#Emergency
#Police
#Ebola
#EbolaVirus
#army
#Virus
#FluVirus
#Flu.
#The End
#Zombie
#Zombies
#Thisistheend
#Armageddon
#Apocalypse
#Terroristattack
#Looting
#Riots
#TerrorAlert
#Flesh eaters
#Thewalkingplague

#CoughingupBlood
#CattleFlu
#Sick
#Crazy
#Fluvirus
#Mysteryfluvirus
#Zombiewar
#Rabies
#Dead
#Police
#Army
#MERS
#999
#Death
#911
#Emergency
#Help
#helpMe
#TheWalkingDead
#Pandemic
#FluPandemic
#TheDeadWalk
#Plague
#MutatedEbolaVirus
#WordWarThree
#Dying
#CJDmadcowdisease
#NoGoZone
#Goodbyemom

This is just what I have found in the last half hour online. There's nothing outside my window here in New Jersey (though it always looks bleak out there)people arguing, shouting and loud sirens. To be honest I'm too scared to go and investigate.

#100
Zomboid
Guest
October 10th : 2019

They're Here!
The Zombies are here!
It finally came true!

#101
Discare
Guest
October 10th : 2019

@Amy That is shocking
For once the latest tween wannabies and celebrities are not the biggest trending news story and it's nice not to see Twerk being the most popular Tag.
On a serious note we're getting out and away from the city, we are on push bikes, the roads are gridlocked.
It's mayhem we have to leave our dog cany behind, I'm so worried and hope she will be okay.

#102
Prepper Max
Member
Moderator
October 10th : 2019

There are reports of London bridge being destroyed and

rumours of terror attacks. Other rumours say that they are trying to contain the virus within the centre of London. The streets of London now look like a massacre from a horror film.

Get yourself in a safe place/location with fresh clean supply of water and food for and enough for a good while.

#103
Baxxa12
Guest
October 10th : 2019

Please if anyone is reading this help us, where are the police?
When is help coming?
We are in Clacton Essex!
we are all in the amusements on the pier itself there is about thirty of us here...
Please help us now!!!!!!

#104
Reece
Member
October 10th : 2019

Now the Term Cattle flu has officially disappeared from the news broadcasts. The virus now is "unidentified" because of the causes and affects it has on the body. The words Rabies/Ebola and Avian Flu if flying around at the moment, quite a bit.
This does seem like it could really be a form of rabies!

#105
Stanley
Member
October 10th : 2019

They're telling you on the news channels to stay inside and wait to hear from your local authorities to come to you. Here in the United Kingdom they're saying that anyone in the centre of London who is preset on the street will be shot unless they have official reason for being there.

#106
Reece
Member
October 10th : 2019

London's burning! The millennium bridge is gone and white tents and quarantine facilities are popping up all over the place. I'm in surrey, the United Kingdom and its crazy, it's like a mini riot out there and I'm quite a way away from the town center.

#107
Vaderz12
Guest
October 10th : 2019

Me and my wife are going to walk to my aunt's cabin. We can't carry too much, but we are what people call prepared. We have all the basics and yes, we have a gun. The infection is causing zombie like effects do not, I repeat stay in the cities.

#108
JJ
Member
October 10th : 2019

I always thought it would be a global economic crisis that would hit us or overpopulation that would end it all, not a bloody zombie apocalypse; if it is zombie like beings I'll kill the lot of them!

#109
Prepper Max
Member
Moderator
October 10th : 2019

I have just spent some time while I still can making use of the internet! Looking up flu pandemics.
During the 1918 Flu pandemic:
–Approx. 20% – 40% of the worldwide population became ill
–As an estimate around fifty million people died all over.
During the 2009-2010 Flu pandemic:
–It is estimated that between forty million to ninety million people actually had the H1N1 between 2009 and 2010.
–And an estimated death rate of   between 8,870 and 18,300 from the H1N1 virus.
–The H1N1 was the last known pandemic to hit, and if over ninety million people were carrying this virus you can't tell me it has nothing to do with this, viruses are clever they are bastards.
I know this does not really help, in the end they are zombie like beings full of rage!

The number of Cannibal attacks is of the chart!

110
Stanley
Member
October 10th : 2019

There are reports that hundreds of people are becoming brain dead due to complications with this strain of flu.
Yeah, look around arse-holes it's not hard to see why there is a walking plague out there.

#111
Daz
Member
October 10th : 2019

The end is nigh its official.

I work in the military sector and can tell you that we are officially losing the battle. We were promised back up from other countries but it never arrived.
All the training I've done and all the sights I've seen couldn't prepare me for this.
Stay safe!
Stay inside!
We are in the process of getting civilians into safe camps across the country.
If you have to fight them aim for the head and don't get too close.

#112
Gerty
Member
October 10th : 2019

Can't they just quarantine everyone who has this and separate us the healthy lot?
Surely that would be easier!

#113
James21
Member
October 10th : 2019

That would be a good idea, they should have thought of that. The airports are closed everywhere, we were due to go on our holidays. No money as we just changed our currency over and nowhere to go. We are not even allowed to wait inside the airport as they say it's a health and safety risk. Banks are reporting problems with sending and receiving money.

#114
Prepper Max
Member
Moderator
October 10th : 2019

The only way to kill a zombie or someone infected with the virus is to destroy the brain.

This is the only way to kill them, until the brain is completely destroyed they will still keep coming for you. Don't waste time and energy attacking any other body part of the zombie just aim for the brain

You must get out of town; a large populated city is the worst place you could possibly be when this is going down. The further that you get away from civilization the better, big cities and towns are a no no, get the hell out of there as quick as you can. Be ready to leave with your bug-out bag in tow to your planned destination as safely and as quit as possible. Blend in, keep unnoticed where possible, and if you are alone be sure to keep looking back in case you are being followed and you are entering a vulnerable situation.

A strong defence is the best defence. Remember defence is such a huge part of your plan and survival. Without a strong defence against the undead and rogue survivors you are dead. You will need to defend everything. It is ideal to have someone on lookout duty all the time, taking it in shifts, as this will be both mentally and physically tiring. Whoever is on guard duty will need to have a main defence weapon and a at least one other back up weapon preferably two.

Where will you go?

Don't just walk aimlessly into an even worse situation than you may already be in!

What will you eat?

If you are staying indoors – plan and the same goes for traveling!

Where is your closest source of water?

Have you got enough water?

Is the water safe to drink?

Defend yourself and don't trust anyone!

#115
Lynne
Guest
October 10th : 2019

Prepare yourself this is now serious, get some food and safe drinking water ready (I'm not drinking anything from a tap) I strongly advise everyone else not too either!

#116
Reg
Guest
October 10th : 2019

I'm sitting in my London flat looking out from the Thames, there must be six or seven helicopters up at the moment. I know we're used to sirens but they have not stopped all day, something big is happening!
This is it!

#117
Terry
Member
October 10th : 2019

I've just filmed whatever you call people who bite one another; this is absurd there was a body on the floor and someone was literally ripping skin, guts, organs and eating it like it was a steak.

#118
JamesTK
Member
October 10th : 2019

'The dead are walking'

This is everywhere, on the radio, even talks on the news channel.

We are all proper fucked!

#119
Macky
Member
October 10th : 2019

When the dead walk the earth, I don't.

Simple as that!

Goodbye world!

#120
ConcernedMum
Guest
October 10th : 2019

Every school here in the United Kingdom is now officially closed. They sent a text message for me to pick up my son over an hour ago, I was on my way to get him, but I work far away, so my brother has picked him up and he is safe but very scared. There's a sign I just passed at the hospital saying no admittance and they have security outside and a massive line of angry and injured people fighting with each other to get to the front of the queue.

How is this all happening so quick?

#121
Jaimie
Guest
October 10th : 2019

Only god knows how and why!
I'm in Australia,
Same here!
All transport has stopped from Victoria to Sydney, It's at a standstill and all I can see from my window is smoke, smashed cars and a large bus on its side. I don't know what to do for the best; no one is taking control here. I did see one army bus taking passengers and kids on to it but I don't know what it's about. I assume they are taking people to these safe camps/fema camps? Maybe it's like the arc or something but I'm scared to shit and really freaked out. This is like a really bad nightmare but worse! I can't stop shaking!

#122
Prepper Max
Member
Moderator
October 10th : 2019

Don't join a group you will have a better chance of surviving own, other people will slow you down, plus who can really trust again?

No matter how much you can be prepared you can never really be prepared for something like this!

#123
Adam S
Guest
October 10th : 2019

We are in Phoenix Arizona here and yes there is trouble. I don't know to what extent, there's nothing outside my window directly but the news is mainly about the virus and the attacks, there is a huge airborne military presence and sirens can be heard.

I'm locking myself indoors and getting as much food and drink and security sorted while I still can.

#124
JamesTK
Member
October 10th : 2019

Zombies, The dead, The rotter's, the walking dead, the undead, walking cadavers, the walking infected, flesh eaters, The Demons, The Rotten, The Monsters, The Hunted, The Decayed Dead, Biters, Freaks, Ghouls, The Feral's, The Enders, The Rotting Ones, The Rabid, Meat bags, Meat Sacks, whatever you choose to call them.

They are here – its official We are doomed!

#125
Mart
Member

October 10th : 2019

Who would have thought a zombie apocalypse would actually happen in our lifetime?

Zombie is now the most searched term on the internet, there are more and more videos popping up by the second. Unless you're a genius with tons of people from tons of different I.p addresses, then no this is not a hoax. This shit looks real, it feels real, I'm preparing now, and I'm getting my shit together and getting the hell out of here.

Good luck guys don't waste your time on the pc, get out there and get safe, this is bloody it!

#126
Aaylia
Guest
October 10th : 2019

Get a grenade, put it in your hands and pull it!
Who wants to live in a world like this?
Get the fuck off the internet you Dick Heads and fucking Run like hell!

#127
Kaydan
Guest
October 10th : 2019

Fuck Her!
I'm a survivor!
I'm safe here, Well safe enough!
They're saying that it's a flu, but from what I have witnessed it looks like a form of Haemorrhagic Fever. I'm not the only one who thinks so either, there are so many reports online saying this is a form of Haemorrhagic Fever caused by a viral infection.

#128
Sandy
Guest
October 10th : 2019

I've just seen a girl in her teens being attacked by a boy three feet away from me. I kicked the attacker then it came for me, I was lucky I got away. Please take this seriously, all this is real!!
What do we do for the best? I'm, scared to death!

#129
Jonny
Member
October 10th : 2019

@Sandy
Get out of the cities.

Cover your mouth at all times and carry a weapon with you if you are travelling.

I'm packing a gun, knife and some homemade Molotov Cocktails, plenty of alcohol to drink and food and drink.

#130
Chase
Member
October 10th : 2019

We are being moved out of our homes here in London and told to go with the military we are going to be joining a long line like the fucking pied piper! Surely we are not safe on foot; I assume they can't get a van or truck in the city! The police just pointed go this way and follow then in two's, It's so messed up.
I'm going now with them, I think it's the best bet!
I have no other options...
I have seen people who get bitten they act rabid and in a rage just like the attackers.
Stay Safe everyone.

#131
Zachoria
Member
October 10th : 2019

@Chase
You're right I have witnessed it too, people who get bitten are turning, and they turn within minutes sometimes and sometimes it takes a little longer!
Stockpile weapons, food and ammunition. Damn it stockpiles everything.

#132
petey32
Member
October 10th : 2019

How do we know what is safe to eat or drink and who to get into contact with?
No one is giving us any concrete answers, every site tells a different story.

#133
Zoey
Guest
October 10th : 2019

We're getting ourselves out as well; we are in our family car. We have packed up a few essentials and are just driving, as fast as we can away people are throwing shit at the car it's bloody scarey!

#134
Bizi21
Guest
October 10th : 2019

@Zoey
We are driving too, well trying!
We are on the M25 in the UK but we're at a complete standstill.
We have driven past people looting petrol stations, shops, setting shops on fire and even randomly robbing people who walk past.

The police are nowhere to be seen, it's every man for himself. I'm surprised we still have a phone signal!

#135
Lucia
Guest
October 10th : 2019

There are lots of families nearby here in the US who are getting into underground bunkers; some families are kind enough to let others in.

#136
Chantal
Guest
October 10th : 2019

I'm getting the fuck of here…

#137
Shana17
Member
October 10th : 2019

Be on the lookout for bears, coyotes, cougars and even wolves here in the United States of America. If you are about to head out of the city think and be well armed, don't escape from the city thinking that you will be safe only to end up bait to something else that will be after your flesh, always be on the lookout for everything.
Be on the lookout for the Infected and of course the looters too.

#138
Sydney
Member
October 10th : 2019

Defend yourself at all times from everyone and everything. Never turn your back on them or anyone else during these awful times stay safe all.

#139
Daisy
Member
October 10th : 2019

The armies are closing the streets!
They are even taking some people in vans from certain places, I can't make out if they are injured or fin- so to speak. I have seen what looks like quarantine with people pushed into large white tents, there are people in white and yellow suits with breathing masks all over the place and everyone walking past is covering their mouths going fast about their business. I am in Washington and I'm not leaving my apartment or my dog for anything, it will have to be the end to get me out of here.

#140
Desmond
Member
October 10th : 2019

They are everywhere, we are trying to get out of New York City but the tailbacks are a joke. One of them was banging on the car window it didn't brake but there are bloody hand prints all over the car .We will end up just getting out of the car and walking if this carries on, it's getting worse by the minute here.

#141
Nada Rich
Member
October 10th : 2019

Blow the bastards up, get some TNT, and make some Molotov cocktails. I've killed three in the last hour, they do burn but they keep coming for you, then you can bash their brains out with a baseball bat.
Just DON'T get bitten or Infected by the virus!!!

#142
Prepper Max
Member
Moderator
October 10th : 2019

I have been prepping for any kind of disaster for years. I'm in the United States and we are lucky enough to live in a small populated area, and hold gun licenses!! Out here we are quite safe and secure. I've been on a few websites collecting some helpful info for you all:

The Top Ten essentials to survive the zombie apocalypse:

Water
Food

Defence/weapons
Shelter/base
Fire
First aid kit/medical supplies
Clothing
Light
A plan
Back up weapons

#143
Bap
Guest
October 10th : 2019

This is a hundred percent real, it's no joke. Get out of the cities and built up town but be careful there are gangs on the rampage and looters and arsheoles everywhere.

#144
Peter
Guest
October 10th : 2019

Stop typing everyone and get yourself away from danger, get prepared, get out now and get somewhere safe with water and some food and weapons.
Don't waste your time online!

#145
Lisa
Guest
October 10th : 2019

My friend has just been shot by the police!
We are in Germany, he was running toward the police trying to get away from one of the infected, he was told to stop and put his hands up but he didn't, they hit him straight in the head, he died instantly.
What the hell is going on!

#146
Sandyz
Member
October 10th : 2019

We're here in the United States of America, all I can hear are gunshots from my window. There are hundreds of them now, it's not safe to go outside. We are staying in and boarding up the house as best we can, we have a gun and some ammo, I guess we are the lucky ones.

#147
Clara
Member
October 10th : 2019

There are rumors that there is a reason they are clearing cities. If you are in the city now or major areas get out now!

There are reports of using chemicals, gasses even bombs to get rid of the infected, please get out don't stay.

#148
chillier
Guest
October 10th : 2019

Anyone who is lucky enough to be in a safe-ish area, stay there. Fill your bath tub with water, don't drink tap water there are rumours of terrorists poisoning the water system.

#149
Zombie Girl
Guest
October 10th : 2019

The only way to kill them is to completely destroy the brain of the rabid attackers/Zombie like infected! just don't go killing anyone with a cold or the sniffles, or someone walking like they shat themselves or we will all be fucked.

#150
Dusty
Member
October 10th : 2019

I'm pretty scared, we're being told by the Police to evacuate our homes right now and go with them!
This is serious. This is really happening.
My thoughts and prayers go out to each and every one of you.

#151
Trev678
Guest
October 10th : 2019

@Dusty
Where are you??

#152
Dusty
Member
October 10th : 2019

@Trev678
I am in Pittsburgh, its murder, literally. Cars can't get in or out, sirens, smoke, gunshots, screaming, death that's all there is here...

#153
Tamuan
Guest
October 10th : 2019

A person who is infected with the flu virus can spread it up to six feet away.
Yes six feet away, this is pretty scary stuff!
So imagine how quick this shit will spread!

 # 154
UK Base
Member
October 10th : 2019

We've been picked up by the Army. We're on a bus, we're allowed our cell phones at the moment but they have said that they will collect them up before we reach the base for safety/security reasons. One of the guards mentioned something about the fact that cell phones can be used as detonators to set off bombs.

#155
Romza
Member
October 10th : 2019

I've seen someone become infected with the virus. I saw them change, what the hell is going on? He only began to change a few minutes after being attacked, he lost so much blood, and he died. His muscles were twitching, his eyes turned bloodshot and he started to drool. He became very aggressive and reached out to attack us. I backed away but the man who was sitting next to me on the train was attacked. I didn't hang around long enough to find out what happened next.

#156
AtoZ
Guest
October 10th : 2019

The virus is definitely not airborne, because I've been exposed to infected people and the incubation period is short.

Colleagues at work have turned right in front of my eyes, I got out of there real quick! It's been quite a while now and physically I'm fine though my mental state is a whole different ball game.

#157
Nic
Guest
October 10th : 2019

I'm so scared, they're all dead. My family are all dead.
Help. Help; Help please help me……

#158
Dath
Member
October 10th : 2019

@Nic
Go with the police/army! Find someone of authority.
I guarantee its biochemical weapons causing this.
These camps that are set up all over the globe are rumoured to be test centres please be at least aware of this I would not go near one for all the money or vaccines in the world!

#159
Zim
Member
October 10th : 2019

@Dath I have seen these pics and uploaded clips I don't know if all the Fema camps are that bad but I wouldn't go in one either... IMHO I think they were testing new drugs and maybe a monkey escaped (They always test on things out on monkeys).

#160
Gary56
Guest
October 10th : 2019

Do not leave your house unless told to do so! This is what they said on the news since this morning!
Make your home safe, now while you still can!

#161
Zom55
Member
October 10th : 2019

Every one of them has this rage/aggression. I have seen no exception to this when people that are infected turn.
They *are* Zombies.

#162
Bloge
Member
October 10th : 2019

There is blood everywhere, the first signs of infection are usually coughing blood or showing signs of a fever or both, it seems to vary slightly from person to person.

#163
Gimly
Member
October 10th : 2019

You're right Bloge, my friend had a nose bleed just before turning.
She seemed to almost fit then we managed to isolate her in a room, while she was fitting.
The internet is now as slow as dial up used to be, this page it taking ages to load/refresh!

#164
Kenny
Guest
October 10th : 2019

It is just so crazy out there I've never been so afraid in my whole life as I am now.
We are at work in a supermarket here in Kentucky. We've loaded up food and drink and the workers who are still here are getting into one of the large containers out the back, it's a storage metal crate around ten feet long with a lock, it seems the safest place to be at the moment, I can hear the front windows being smashed as I write this!
When will this wandering sickness end?

#165
Peruthian
Member
October 10th : 2019

@Kenny
It has only just begun!

#166
Caitlin
Member
October 10th : 2019

Bio research has got to be the cause as @Dath suggested, there are have been lots of new facilities popping up owned by Homeland security, and other laboratories have been cropping up all over the place over the last couple of years, more than ever.

 # 167
Stanley
Member
October 10th : 2019

I know in the 60's they were doing controlled tests on LSD. What's to say the controlled just became uncontrollable?

#168
Roger41
Member
October 10th : 2019

I have just had to deal with one of them first hand, someone infected lunged towards my wife. I bashed it to death with a baseball bat, the thing took ages to stop moving, body shots seem to do no damage at all. The brain must be totally destroyed if you want to stand any chance of surviving this horror.
They are Zombie's there is no doubt.

#169
Darly19
Member
October 10th : 2019

The internet is full of rumors that selected people are being taken to Fema Concentration Camps; they're saying this is a good thing and that they are there to help. They are strictly for humanitarian assistance and temporary disaster housing for situations just like this one.
To be honest it sounds like a good idea really, I wish other countries could have been prepared like the United States seems to be, by the way has anyone noticed there has been no official broadcast from the President or the British Prime Minister yet.

#170
Reece
Member
October 10th : 2019

@Darly19
I have seen the websites and even so called selfies from these Fema camps, and yes I do find it very strange the president did not give an official broadcast, there is a fake letter going around meant to be from the president but that's bull shit, you should see all the shit going around there was a letter on a blog from Elvis, Jim Morrison and Bigfoot so don't read too much into it! Not that it would have changed the situation it really is every man for himself out there.

#171
Caitlin
Guest
October 10th : 2019

Viruses can normally only replicate in living cells. The standard influenza virus binds through hemagglutinin directly into sialic acid sugars onto the surfaces of epithelial cells, most commonly to the lungs, nose and throat — So why are there rumours of the Dead Rising From Their Graves!???

#172
Zed1
Guest
October 10th : 2019

I never really looked at it like that before!

I am in Wales, We are in a desolate area so to speak, there are people around but we are spread out. I'm staying here at my home. I've boarded up the windows.

My wife has just returned from the city, at first I thought she just had a cold coming. She had a high fever but I wasn't surprised, after all she'd been travelling on those germ infested tube trains around the city, but within the hour she was coughing up blood and starting to hallucinate. I saw her turn, she became aggressive toward me, and it just wasn't her anymore. I watched as her features became contorted with a rage burning inside of her. I tried my best to restrain her, but she seemed to have acquired a relentless strength, when restraining proved futile I had no option, I had to kill her.

I don't want to be alive anymore, without her it will just be an existence even if all this madness goes away but I have to stay strong for my son, I have to ensure his safety. I have had no response from my calls to him. Is anyone on here in Ireland, could you please let me know how the situation is progressing there. I will continue to pray for his safety.

Be safe everyone

#173
Who knows
Member
October 10th : 2019

There have been reports of terrorist attacks over the past few months, more than ever, it must have something to do with it!

Were we not on green alert already checking into the airport last month seemed to take forever and I think having no luggage on board even a handbag or drinks was taking it too far! Or was it? This is a Terrorist attack for sure!

#174
Charles13
Member
October 10th : 2019

I'm scared about getting the Cattle Flu or whatever it's called now, or bitten by one of them. This flu epidemic's the worst in history.

#175
Zletters
Member
October 10th : 2019

Be careful out there!
Watch out for the walking dead and looters too.
I nearly got hit by a falling helicopter! This is so messed up guys;
I think I'm dreaming or something.
It is definitely a nightmare!

#176
Tony
Member
October 10th : 2019

I wonder if they are fast or slow zombies.
They have to be slow ones really; no one likes the fast ones do they. It's always the mistakes that a bunch of survivors make that sod it up in the end, though it makes for an entertaining watch. I do hope these are slow; it would be over quicker if they were fast

though! There are no walking dead here yet just looters and riots.

#177
Kerry
Guest
October 10th : 2019

@Tony
The infected who are rabid/aggressive are slow, they stumble, they are in no way steady on their feet, use this to your advantage.

#178
Jimm
Member
October 10th : 2019

This is really happening, I have just witnessed here in the city of Norwich, A man attacking a young child. I just ran home, he started attacking a lady who intervened there was blood every-where. I'm getting out as soon as I can, this is real!!!!!!! Please do the same get to safety, this is the end.

#179
Shifty
Guest
October 10th : 2019

If they are zombies, then aim for the head.

#180
Zark
Member
October 10th : 2019

I have seen from my window a woman literally biting a man and taking a chunk out of him and chewing it, there is blood all over the pavement and I had to close the window because of the screaming. The reality is that I don't know if they are, as you say, zombies but there is some virus or something causing people to go rabid and bite one another. I'm locking the house up and securing everything here please do the same; I promise this is not a joke. Something big and nasty is going down.

#181
Buzz
Member
October 10th : 2019

I'm in the sticks out here in Oregon, not too much to report out here. The sky is full of helicopters and planes going over and I've never seen so many birds! The news channels are reporting the Flu warning of high fever, temperature, headaches and coughing blood or nose bleeds. There are even videos online and the news channel is even saying this could be terrorist warfare attack, but I can't see anything unusual from my window or anything.
The videos are of real zombie like people.
I know for a fact that the virus has reached Northern Maine, Nebraska and Arizona from talking to friends! So it won't be long till it spreads here!
Don't think because you are in the sticks that you are safe, in fact

the opposite as everyone is trying to get to places like this thinking they are safe but everyone has the same idea!

#182
Birdy
Member
October 10th : 2019

They do look like zombies, there is so much footage of people attacking and feasting on flesh for them not to be.
I don't believe it will be the end or anything.
This will be controlled!
There are reports around China of a very contagious flu. That's all that's being broadcast on the news here. It's mayhem, people already wear masks in the street but now they're wearing hazmat suits. I work here in China as a teacher, I'm originally from England. They are obsessed with germs out here, it did take me a while to adjust to the masks, it was kind of freaky at first, I just got used to the smog and germs, I suppose.
But yes something is happening here too!

183
Leilaz
Guest
October 10th : 2019

We were becoming over-populated; this is a very clever way of stopping it, though not humane!
I really think this was man made!
It's one way of wiping out freeloaders!
A zombie apocalypse could just do that!

#184
Bazza
Member
October 10th : 2019

There are reports here on the news channels of incidents all over which, like the above poster said of mystery flu like virus, mystery attacks and even rioting, looting, cannibalistic attacks and bombings.

#185
1842
Guest
October 10th : 2019

Wild, dark times are rumbling toward us, and the prophet who wishes to write a new apocalypse will have to invent entirely new beasts, and beasts so terrible that the ancient animal symbols of St. John will seem like cooing doves and cupids in comparison. HEINRICH HEINE

#186
Stanley
Member
October 10th : 2019

I have to go deal with some dickheads at the door, these looters or raiders whatever you call them do have some front.
They are trying to get in I just heard the back window smash, I will kill these fuckers…

#187
PrepperMax
Member
Moderator
October 10th : 2019

Trying to find as many safety tips as possible that I have in my Prepper notes that will relate to this crisis!

There's no point crying or getting depressed, pull your shit together, get yourself in a functional, positive mind-set. This sounds harsh but you are a survivor. You are a zombie hunter – get out there and kill some zombie ass.

Don't even think for a minute that you will be safe behind glass you won't be! Don't sit or let children play behind glass The infected and rogue survivors will go straight through it. Board up every window as soon as possible.

In any crisis people will start to change

Every person across the globe will change. Expect this! Even the people who used to be shy will now be crazed killers. The old shop keeper now will be a killer, focused on trying to secure his precious cargo. The young mum will do anything to protect her baby and to get it the right amount of food or drink. She will kill anyone who gets in her way.

Don't depend on anyone!
This is so true!

You will not be able to depend on the emergency services, it doesn't matter which one you are after: the police, fire services the army, ambulances, they will all be gone. Be prepared to deal with things yourself as best you can. You have no option now. Even if the government and emergency services have the best intentions they could never deal with a virus spreading at this rate. The rate this thing spread at means that big and small cities could be gone in hours. More people equal more zombies.

Use daylight wisely.

Daylight is your friend. People will attack day or night but you can see them better in the day light, Plan, prepare, and know where you will be when it is dark.

Please keep all your meds with you at all times whatever you decide to do or wherever you decide to go. Carry your asthma inhalers or any tablets you need to take with you. It has been advised on one site to carry passports and ID with you. In some countries there is no admission to the Fema camps without them. I personally do not trust a soul and would not go into one of these camps but the decision is with you. The best thing you can do is lock up, board up, have enough food and water and try to wait this out. I would even try to board up the windows and doors. Keep lights off and even try to seal the windows so fumes or contaminated air cannot come in the house.

Don't forget to ration your food out, you don't know how long you will be inside for.

If you only have tap water available then you have no option but to drink it, so the best thing to do is boil the water first. This should make the water safe to drink.

It is not advised to eat any wild animals during any pandemic. You don't know which animals have been infected or even exposed to radiation, but if you find yourself in a life or death situation and you have no other choice, go for underground animals first, like rabbits. They will have less chance of being contaminated. Birds and fish will have a higher chance of conta-mination.

#188
Trust
Member
October 10th : 2019

Be careful Stanley, stay safe.
Good advice @PrepperMax!
Is this the big bang that will end it all, I knew it started with one,
I just didn't think it would end with one?
There are so many stories on message boards od whole towns,
being literally blown up just to try to contain the virus!
I've seen things you would not ever in your life want to witness,
let alone see in your wildest nightmares. My children are having
to see this, how on Earth do you go back to normality after this?

#189
Brook
Guest
October 10th : 2019

There are now even reports of a mass religious suicide pact. That
is crazy, these aren't suicides, and it clearly is an infection or
chemical warfare causing this.

#190
Kerry
Guest
October 10th : 2019

It really is happening. I have just seen as an attack in front of my eyes, a young teenager bit his friend and tried to carry on biting him. Some people intervened then they got bitten too, the first one who got bitten went into shock or something, they were in a state on the floor then out of nowhere he started to do the same trying to bite people I wasn't close enough to see exactly what happened next but I got the hell out of there. It seems whatever virus this is it causes a rage, you go rabid and bite and attack people.

This is unreal!

Everyone is running and panicking, this shit is real! I don't know what to do for the best.

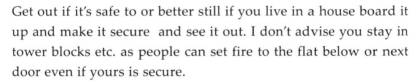

#191
Tony
Member
October 10th : 2019

Get out if it's safe to or better still if you live in a house board it up and make it secure and see it out. I don't advise you stay in tower blocks etc. as people can set fire to the flat below or next door even if yours is secure.

#192
Finlay
Guest
October 10th : 2019

H1N1 virus reached epidemic levels in the US that was the news in early 2014 through online news not on the TV so to speak.

It did say at the time that the H1N1 virus was mainly killing young adults and the middle aged.

You can't tell me the H1N1 virus has nothing to do with this.

Viruses are very complex

The virus itself is not alive

The Viruses themselves need to enter a human or animal cell, they will take over the cell to help them multiply. Most viruses may also infect bacterial cells. The virus particle attaches to a host cell.

#193
Callum
Member
October 10th : 2019

@Finlay

Good point it could be, Viruses really seem to be very complex indeed and it will take some time I assume for them to provide us with a vaccine.

#194
Stanley
Member
October 10th : 2019

I've been bitten, right on the bloody shoulder; by one of the bastards I'm going to take down as many of them as I can.

#195
Reece
Member
October 10th : 2019

So sorry to hear that,

Go get them Stanley, my good friend.
You go kill as many of them as you possibly can.
Don't give up...

#196
Ashton
Member
October 10th : 2019

Do hand sanitizers like alcohol based ones work, and stop you from getting the flu? I know that they always have them in hospitals now before you go into a ward. Would drinking neat vodka prevent you from getting it?

 # 197
Billi34
Guest
October 10th : 2019

@Ashton
I don't think drinking neat alcohol could stop it but damn I need a drink!
They are advising us to use hand sanitizers.
It's a bit fucking late for that!
No way is some Alcohol rub going to stop this!

#198
Prepper Max
Member
Moderator
October 10th : 2019

@Stanley if you have been bitten/infected you may still have a chance, if you have been bitten on the lower arm hand or leg immediately remove that part of the body to try to stop the infection spreading through the blood stream, I've watched a video that was just uploaded of someone doing this and they had a live cam on them for five minutes after and apart from being in pain and feeling faint from loss of blood and shock they were at least successful in not turning into a rabid monster.

#199
Sebastian
Member
October 10th : 2019

When would a pandemic virus end? I know most viruses go on for years afterwards, looking at it this way it is really scary.

#200
Aidan
Member
October 10th : 2019

@Sebastian
This one could go on and mutate, this is a bastard. I'm more scared of actually getting the virus inside me than getting bitten. At least you can see the zombie's coming for you, the tiny droplets of the virus out of someone's nose or saliva are invisible to the naked eye.

#201
Brad32
Member
October 10th : 2019

If we are healthy, do you reckon we will have less of a chance actually getting the virus, I hope so at least.

#202
Aidan
Member
October 10th : 2019

@Brad32
They did say that the old, people who already had health issues or young would be more at risk at the start but that was when they thought it was just a standard flu they were dealing with. To be honest I don't think it matters, if you were Mr. Universe and you get bitten by one of them you're going down, simple as that.

#203
Bert
Member
October 10th : 2019

Can you catch this flu? I mean is this airborne? Or would you have to go in direct contact with someone who has the virus itself? Then have an incubation or dormant phase, I'm really worried I have a very young daughter who has recently got back from playschool. I'm so worried and I don't know what to do, I phoned the doctors they said there are reports of a dreadful Flu like virus, they don't know the details and said look and listen to the news, apparently the surgery is mayhem there is a queue so far down the road there are even police and security there.

#204
Bubba
Member
October 10th : 2019

The Zombie Virus has gone Viral!
There are rumors that people who haven't been bitten are coming back to life as the infected. I haven't seen it first hand, so I'm not sure if it's true or not.
I don't know what to believe anymore, this is all so unreal.

#205
Kevlarz1
Guest
October 10th : 2019

Every one of you is going to die, and you sit here chatting, I've just come on here to tell you...
You fuckers better watch out the Hoodyazee are ere!! Were a Gang and anyone gets in our way boom its peak!

We gonna run this city!

Just wait and see...

206
Petra
Member
October 10th : 2019

@Kevlarz1
Think you're tough online. Your little lot will get wiped out first, my husband is a member of the SAS and yes they are equipped for zombies and dickheads like you!
Every gang will get wiped out along with the zombies. This way all the vermin will be washed away in one swoop!
No looters are safe trust me! From anyone! Have you not seen the videos of the people going around taking the law in their own hands? Where there is no law these people of 100 strong are going around shooting and putting an end to not only the zombies but vigilante style and yes people like you must have a Death Wish...?

#207
Helen
Guest
October 10th : 2019

I agree but I think the SAS are more equipped to deal with gangs than they are zombies, just look around you!
They are everywhere; I'm getting out while I still can.
Run!
The police are being overthrown by them; there is absolutely no control here!

#208
Zombie Hunter
Member
October 10th : 2019

@Kevlarz1
No reply I thought not!!

#209
Joshua
Member
October 10th : 2019

Basically we're all screwed!
I'm making weapons from everything here. good job I've got a garden shed full of tools and power drills, chainsaws all fully charged.
I have heard rumors that Mosquitoes are carrying the virus, is there any truth to this?

#210
Caitlin
Member
October 10th : 2019

@J They might be carrying the virus now it's everywhere!
If they did manage to make a vaccine I wouldn't touch it with a barge pole. I would take my chances, there's no way they could have enough time to test it out, and I'm not being any ones guinea pig.

If the vaccine comes out stay away from it!

I didn't go near it in 2009 with swine flu, I have chest problems breathing and I don't even have my flu shot.

#211
Caitlin
Member
October 10th : 2019

I have seen what looks like a zombie well lots of them, from my flat window in New York City!

The streets from both sides are closed and they are trying to capture them, they look like a normal people really just covered in blood and almost dragging its body really slow.

I don't think this has sunk in yet I'm, Numb!

 # 212
Barney
Member
October 10th : 2019

This is making me feel sick to my stomach I can't stop shaking, I'm in Canada here and yes there are reports of attacks and illnesses here.

Is this the end of Everything? Fuck I wish I did more with my life...

#213
JohnE
Member
October 10th : 2019

They have cornered our street off, we are in Sweden and they are now telling us to get out safely from the city on the police's authority.

#214
Joe
Member
Moderator
October 10th : 2019

We were called to collect our children from school after the number of infected rose dramatically throughout the day.
We ran to the school, I collected Jake from the assembly hall but Mandy was running round screaming frantically, She couldn't find her son Ben. She was told by one of the teaching assistants that her son had been taken ill just minutes before we got there. He was in quarantine, but it was too late.
Then we heard the gunshots from the police her son was shot directly in the head, I can still hear her blood curdling scream.
We are at home now and locked up waiting further instruction we are turning everything off not to attract unwanted attention as advised by the police, the police officer from the school did say they are working on something and to wait at home…
Doesn't seem to be working, whatever it was…
Good luck all,
Fight back!

#215
Sammy43
Member
Moderator
October 10th : 2019

I witnessed an elderly lady devouring flesh from a victim on the floor. Anyone of any age can and will turn but nothing can prepare you for seeing a young child turn into one of them. I don't know what was worse, watching a child trying to attack a man or the man ending the child's life.

#216
Newman79
Member
Moderator
October 10th : 2019

It proves how little I know about the human body, how on earth can the brain stay active when the heart is literally ripped from the chest and the spine itself if removed?
Even when I witnessed a gang decapitate a zombie the head continued to move with the mouth biting right up until the brain was destroyed.

#217
Pepper Max
Member
Moderator
October 10th : 2019

Thank you all for your help everyone!
It's carnage here!
I'm going in the bunker soon, good luck everyone!

#218
Zombie Hunter
Member
October 10th : 2019

Stay on rooftops, they don't really know or have the ability to climb up high. Trees are good, stay on top of buildings until help comes, remember this. This may just save your life.

 # 219
Rusty
Member
October 10th : 2019

I just saw my best friend turn into one of those things!
That's not going to be me,
No way am I going to end up that way!

#220
Kirk
Member
October 10th : 2019

I am literally stuck between stations, the train is at a standstill between London and Scotland. I'm so, so worried!
I was told of an attack that has gotten out of control in the underground, apparently all of the trains and public transport have

been stopped.

#221
Dixie
Guest
October 10th : 2019

I have seen videos of rotting corpses rising from graveyards! Are these real or fake?
Call me stupid but if this was the case then it would have started from the zombies that had risen from their graves. For some reason then they bite, infect and so on, but if not how could the infection be contracted by the dead? Possibly a time frame? I know that maybe the last thing to worry about just really trying to make some sense out of all this craziness!

#222
Hubert
Guest
October 10th : 2019

This is Z-Day!
This is the end!
I will stand against them, I will fight for my family and friends, and I will die for every one of them. If I die protecting or saving someone's life, my life it will not be a life lost in vain.

#223
Kirt666
Member
October 10th : 2019

You all know that the probability of surviving this is slim to none, right??????
You will all die.
It doesn't matter where you are or who you are!

#224
RonP
Member
October 10th : 2019

STFU– Kirt666

So much for positive thinking you're doomed from the start with that attitude.

#225
Richiec
Guest
October 10th : 2019

Get yourself to the nearest army barracks and get in a tank, lock that door and just stay there.

#226
Regan
Guest
October 10th : 2019

I'm going to kill the bastards with my chainsaw if they come into my home, I'm quicker than they are, and I'm faster and smarter watch out.

They are slow moving once infected...

#227
Pichit
Guest
October 10th : 2019

I'm in Amsterdam we're getting out of the cities and towns. We are walking by foot as cars, trains and trams are at a standstill.

#228
Campbell
Guest
October 10th : 2019

Do animals Carry the virus? Can they transmit it through a bite etc.?

#229
RonP
Member
October 10th : 2019

@Campbell
I have seen quite a few dead animals around, but have not seen any immediate signs of infected animals.
But I would not go near any animals that is just my opinion.

#230
Jax
Guest
October 10th : 2019

Maybe the animals have a sixth sense they, just know and are moving away. am fortunate enough not to be near a zoo or animal park to find out and don't own any pets.

#231
Kel
Guest
October 10th : 2019

I have a dog, she's is fine at the moment a little shaken due to all the commotion but showing no signs of anything unusual.
Try to stay safe all xxx

#232
Norfolk1
Guest
October 10th : 2019

I and my family live on the Norfolk broads here in the UK. It has kicked off here, people are sick and panicking. I have even witnessed (just five minutes from my house) a lady of around eighty get attacked. I went over but the thing was rabid, his eyes weren't his own, they were red, more than blood shot, he had prominent veins thought his face, he was in a rage. I have now got my family and our elderly neighbor and we have got on to our boat on the river. We are staying in the middle like many people are doing, it seems as if it is the safest place at the moment. I advise anyone to do the same who has the opportunity to.

#233
Tina Zacosy
Guest
October 10th : 2019

Is there a cure? It seems like once you get infected/bitten then you react the same as them, I have witnessed it myself.

#234
RonP
Member
October 10th : 2019

Tina, there is not even a mention of a cure, which is a tad worrying to say the least.

 # 235
carzake
Guest
October 10th : 2019

The News Website has reports of a virus and tells everyone to listen closely to their local radio stations and authorities for their current evacuation guidelines, but does not say directly what the virus Is, how you get it and if is at all treatable. Basically no answers to information that we need to know.

In fact news channels and TV stations are either stopped broadcasting or playing repeats!

#236
Carnage
Member
October 10th : 2019

This makes the recent US, London and France riots seem tame. Saying that it makes world war two look tame, and there are more looters than there are the infected.

#237
Lizbeth
Guest
October 10th : 2019

I'm ready and waiting for them.
Everyone thought I was crazy having two guns in the house...
Who's laughing now!

#238
Geof
Member
October 10th : 2019

What actually started all this?
The government, terrorists or cows? No one seems to know?, on the news it says now each town and state will have their own guidelines and to do as they direct you too for your own safety, from what I can make out if you are in big built up areas with

chance of infection or attacks you need to get out but if you are in the sticks you should stay there and not to enter a city, I've boarded up the doors and windows I have a gun I don't care who tries to come in it could be a zombie a looter it could be the king if he threatens me or my family I will kill him.

#239
Warren
Guest
October 10th : 2019

Get to the countryside or desert, keep hidden, keep down and keep safe.
They do not die/stop from burning them, they do not stop even when you pump a hundred rounds into one of them, and it's useless. Sticking a hatchet in its head is the best way, to finish them.

#240
Zabrinski
Guest
October 10th : 2019

Hawaii is rumored to be the worst effected place, not surprising an Island with that volume of people on!!!

#241
Zombie hunter
Member
October 10th : 2019

MAKE EMERGENCY ESCAPE ROUTES!

They only really die if you destroy the brain, I kicked some lead into one of them (about ten bullets) but the bloody thing continued straight for me. Only aim for the head and don't get their infected blood anywhere near yours.

#242
Hardy
Member
October 10th : 2019

Don't let strangers into your house even if they are sick or wounded, this may sound horrible but I have witnessed rogues going around killing each other for a smoke. Stay safe and don't trust anyone. Think like a vigilante, set up traps all over the house to stop burglars and looters from getting in. If they find it hard to get in they will try somewhere else, keep lights off at night.
It's getting dark here now; it's the best thing to do. Don't draw attention to yourself or your property.

#243
Blake
Member
October 10th : 2019

Thank you all for the info here this seems like a genuine site. I've just been on one forum, the vampire resurrection crew think they are rising, then I went to another site where they said the reptiles are showing their true form!

Why are the government not taking control of this? It really is out of hand now, I have noticed sites all over the net are closing by the minute, or being closed down.

#244
Brazilian
Guest
October 10th : 2019

It is here in Brazil, I'm at the police station with hundreds of others; they're looking after us well here.
My wife is missing, I'm taking it hour by hour here in hope my wife will be safe, there are a lot of evil people in this world but there is also some caring and genuin people who who help others even risking there own lives..I have witnessed this for myself today.

#245
Bitten
Guest
October 10th : 2019

i just been bitten by one of them i killed him as soon as i could it wasnt easy tey are bloody hard to kill
i have a bite on my elbow really worried not a huge bite more like a scratch from the teeth
i beginning to feel a little sick and dizzy but I do'nt know if this is being caused just by me feeling so worried or if I have got it seventeen year old male.

#246
Zombie Hunter
Member
October 10th : 2019

Sorry to hear this...
@Bitten
But as @PrepperMax mentioned...
Cut your bloody arm off immediatly in the hope the infection has not started to spread! This is the only way, you might survive and even this drastic measure is no guarantee.
Buy there aren't many options at this stage!
If you are still there @Bitten act quicky, time is not on your side once you have been bitten!

#247
Shaiv
Member
October 10th : 2019

I'm in Russia,
It's just the same, streets are closed and blood where the once white blanket of snow used to lie.
 It's pure terror outside, internet sites are going down by the second. If you need to get in touch with family and friends for meeting places etc. please do this now. It's all going to shit here very quickly , the news is not even broadcasting anymore, and all the TV stations have completely gone now.

#248
SuellenUS
Guest
October 10th : 2019

I'm gathering up whatever supplies we have indoors " which are very limited" and heading into my basement along with my neighbors, I refused to take their dog as it would attract attention when it barked.

We are just going to try and wait this out "What other choice do we have at this time?"

#249
Catfink
Guest
October 10th : 2019

"Bat Influenza"
There are now rumours that this has stemmed from bat flu.
This is crazy one minute it is caused by something then the next something else... I think we can all agree now knowone knows what the fuck is going on...
I'm on my own and very scrared, like the above post said, I'ts now turning into a waiting game, with a lot of praying and hope that the Government are going to do something to try to restore things as soon as they can!
There's tons of rumours, out there, I'm just boarding the house up and checking the news on TV and online constantly.

#250
Ratty
Guest
October 10th : 2019

We have trawled from Nevada, it is mayhem there!
We are now approaching California and trying to get to the ocean for safety.
Everyone is advising people to get in the ocean even with or without boats I suppose it makes some kind of sense "The Infected" can't swim, I assume they stay in the same state underwater but don't float either, so as long as you don't get into immediate contact with the infected you would be okay, but I don't think I would want to chance it swimming knowing they may be just feet away from you, I don't know what would be worse getting eaten alive by a shark or them!
 I don't know how much luck we will need to get in a boat but if not we shall stay near the water's edge waiting, I don't think crowds of them will be near the water.

#251
Zomboid
Member
October 10th : 2019

I have just witnessed my neighbor getting attacked and eaten right in front of me, we are in the car some clever dick just went passed and smashed the window with a brick.

#252
Mark
Guest
October 10th : 2019

We're in a car on the highway but I don't know where we're headed, we're miles from anywhere.
I'm saying prayers for everyone. I have faith in God; he will protect us. Try to stay safe and not to put yourself in danger.

#253
Baz34
Guest
October 10th : 2019

There are reports across the country that phone lines have been destroyed and the electricity won't last long either. Please contact your relatives and leave notes inside your houses letting others know what route you are going on and how you can meet up later. Tell your loved ones that you love them and give your neighbour a hug. This has happened so fast it's insane! Just witnessed a gun store owner getting shot about a hundred times by a gang of youths, to me the kids and the rioting is scarier than the infected.

#254
Faye
Member
October 10th : 2019

The infected are everywhere! People are turning by the second! We are getting out, does anyone know where truly is safe?

255
Bob44
Member
October 10th : 2019

@Faye
No it's a game of chance, we're taking our camping stuff and getting the hell out away from everyone.
"Heard good things about parts of wales and even places becoming like a mini Glastonbury no not the music but community spirit helping each other out camping sharing food and even building barricades between them and the wandering dead."

#256
Attica
Guest
October 10th : 2019

We have just passed a graveyard, there are tons of them and groups of tourists who think it's a joke. This are weird shit! I don't understand why and how can you get this virus? Why are people turning? Why are they biting people? What caused this? Maybe no one knows.

#257
JRMontell
Member
October 10th : 2019

They are everywhere here!
This has brought out not only the nutters but the usual brigade of trouble-makers. All the shops in the village have been looted and then torched we have no weapons to defend ourselves here we are really scared; we are locking ourselves indoors here.
But how long will we be safe for?

#258
Zombie Hunter
Member
October 10th : 2019

They are walking quite slowly, if you zig-zag around them and don't walk in straight lines it freaks them out They won't come straight for you, watch out as above for looters, there are no law here either.
Shoot them in the head, or better put an axe or a machete through it, that should slow them down.

#259
Robot
Guest
October 10th : 2019

The virus is out of control, its spreading at such a fast rate. I have contacted my son he said he is in a safe zone with the army; apparently they are taking people slow and steady into army bases maybe head to them if you have the chance.

#260
Angelina
Member
October 10th : 2019

#Helpmeplease i dont know what to do and im in my flat in London in Brixton its total carnage out there
i cant leave there are too many of them they are trying to get in im freaked out here

#261
Robin458
Guest
October 10th : 2019

I'm in Washington USA, the Whitehouse is on fire literally, there are videos of this all over the net already. I thought it was a hoax but when you see this up-close it's freaky, everyone has been told to leave. Does this mean they have won already?

#262
Pete Cork
Guest
October 10th : 2019

I'm in Belfast
I can't get into contact with any of my family; I think the lines are

down their end. Mum, Dad its Pete Cork if you see this I'm staying where I am, I hope Galway is safe I LOVE YOU.

#263
Dagon
Guest
October 10th : 2019

I'm in Devon,
We are heading out to sea in a boat with some others who have kindly let us join them. There was mayhem at the harbour, people being not only bitten but attacked by the general public and hundreds trying to get on board any boats that could. There are even people getting in inflatable's and surfboards and rubber rings to get away from them.

#264
Marco
Guest
October 10th : 2019

I'm in Italy, I'm currently in Pescara we are heading for the ocean too. It's going to be the only safe bet; areas have already been bombed by either the government or terrorists. People have risen from the dead; they walk slowly but have a lot of strength. I just saw one with no legs pulling itself over to a body on the floor then feasting.

#265
Steph123
Guest
October 10th : 2019

Here in Maine we are all trying to get to the ocean too but many others have had the same idea so be quick. All you can see is blood and remains of the living and the dead just scattered around.

#266
Petera1234
Member
October 10th : 2019

Romania is a living dead hell hole; it's a bloody war zone Here!

WE ARE ALL JUST SITTING DUCKS WAITING TO BE KILLED.

#267
Charnel
Member
October 10th : 2019

Osaka Japan is the same, we are being ushered to safe zones now, we are being put into quarantines first it's kind of scary.

#268
Gaeta687
Guest
October 10th : 2019

I'm in New Zealand it's here now; we are being informed of attacks by the government now from all over the globe too.

#269
Groggy
Guest
October 10th : 2019

They're telling everyone to get out of cities; do they not realize the infected will be in these areas too? The forests and bushy areas will be the worst, they will be harder to see, and this is crazy.

#270
Zombie Hunter
Member
October 10th : 2019

Surround yourself with fat people and people who are slower and less fit than you at least you will be the last one to go.
JK– But it could work!

#271
Georges
Member
October 10th : 2019

We were lucky enough to get in a boat from Arizona, we have landed in Hawaii. We are at a police station with many others in the same boat (so to speak) it's a war zone here but at least there's more control here than in the US.

#272
DRS
Member
October 10th : 2019

Kansas, Nebraska, Wyoming and the surrounding areas are all infected; they're trying to quarantine and close down areas here too. We can see people's homes on fire.
@Georges
You are silly going to a small island I'd stay on the boat if I were you!

 # 273
Bat3490
Member
October 10th : 2019

Be sure not to get scratched by the Infected, I witnessed someone who got scratched; they turned the same as if they had been bitten by one.

#274
Dave19
Member
October 10th : 2019

I'm in Wales here, our phones are going by the second and all tube sharing sites and major social networks have officially gone, this will not be here long guys!

#275
WainwrightJr
Member
October 10th : 2019

Everyone here is heading for high ground, there are groups of hundreds all sticking together, it seems like safety in numbers is the best way.

#276
MarcelaQ
Member
October 10th : 2019

Mexico is no more, it's a mass of demolition and smoke, I work with the army but this is hell.
People running screaming and crying men woman and children all dying!
I feel helpless and sick as I can do nothing!

 # 277
Kath KAT
Guest
October 10th : 2019

Be sure to have enough supplies on you whilst travelling and ensure that you have enough water and food for a few days and appropriate clothing. My prayers are with every one of you, God bless.

#278
Clayton
Member
October 10th : 2019

I have all I need during this time. I have enough medicines to kill myself. I refuse to be a test subject or to be eaten alive, I have my dignity it may not be a lot but it stands for something with me. Bless you all.

#279
Stephaney
Member
October 10th : 2019

We are gathering supplies and weapons here in Scotland; there are a small team of us. We are even making weapons out of knives and broom handles, anything where you don't have to get into close contacted with them is ideal. Arm yourselves.

#280
Carnie23
Guest
October 10th : 2019

The best advice –Get the Hell out of Dodge. While you still can.

#281
Brandonx3
Member
October 10th : 2019

We have been told by a police officer to pair up.
Everyone here now has a partner and we have to walk and stay in pairs at all times. I don't know where they are leading us or where this so called safe zone is but if I get there I will tell you, if the internet is still up.

#282
Evan Smith
Member
October 10th : 2019

They don't seem to get tired, I'm buggered!
They keep coming at you no matter what. I have just had more than a lucky escape here in the office.

#283
Helps
Member
October 10th : 2019

#help
Somebody please help us!
We are trapped in the basement at the St Paul's cathedral in central London there are seven of us here two of which are seriously injured and losing blood by the second. I have a broken ankle and one of the groups has been stabbed, the others have been attacked and even bitten. We are in need of immediate assistance and medical help but we can't get through to 999, we've been trying for ages on hold Please pass this information on to the authorities, there are hundreds of them out there we have no way of getting out of here please help us!

#284
Zombie Hunter
Member
October 10th : 2019

@Helps

I have left your message on the police website and on the forum there that as of a few seconds ago was still up, I wish you well and hope help will come soon.

#285
Mel43
Guest
October 10th : 2019

I and my husband have been doing the same; we have a baseball bat and an assortment of kitchen knives and a rather blunt decorative samurai sword. The electric is still on, so I have even kept boiling the kettle so that if we get looters I can chuck it over their heads. We have arranged garden house bricks and the like upstairs under every window that way if anyone tries to get in we can try to stop them by dropping bricks on them. I even found some lighter fluid that can be used and petrol to set any of them on fire.

#286
Dark star
Member
October 10th : 2019

I have an axe, shovel, broken china, glass and a baseball bat to protect myself. I'm not leaving my house for no one, oh and I have the most important thing, a large litre bottle of bourbon.

#287
ZombieNightmare
Guest
October 10th : 2019

It's true

"The Dead Have inherited the earth."
"What a bunch of sad nerds get off here! now and man up!!
Are you all really this mental?

#288
Worried Mum
Member
October 10th : 2019

How can I get a prescription for my daughters Asthma inhaler? It has about one puff left in it, we were due to collect the prescription in the morning, and I'm really worried. No pharmacies or surgeries are even open, 999 are less than useless and the last time she was without her spray she had to be hospitalized. Stress seems to make her worse,
I am a really worried mother,
someone please help,
I am in Ontario.

#289
Zombie Hunter
Member
October 10th : 2019

@ZombieNightmare "Yes you still get arsholes like you even in these times, at least you will finally be cut from mummy's apron strings!"

@WorriedMum
If the worst comes to the worst try getting her to breathe in through a paper bag. Drink at least a large glass of water and strong coffee is also good for asthma. Try to get her as calm and

relaxed as possible, reassurance and slow deep breaths,
I wish you all the best.

#290
Susan Farmer
Guest
October 10th : 2019

The hospital here in Australia is a corpse's graveyard now.
I was working as an orderly in the hospital, we hadn't heard of
any problems or even rumors this morning but then it happened.
It happen so quickly we couldn't establish any order at all, it was
insane. Corpses just came to life, I thought at first you had to be
bitten but it seems like an infection that by now we will all have.
When we tried to contain the corpses they came back to life,
suddenly there appearance changed and they were no longer in
charge of their bodies, something else was in control. These are
now rabid creatures with no respect for life, do not I repeat not
get close to them and don't let them bite you or you *will* die and
turn into one of them. I haven't heard or seen anything like this
in my life.

#291
Dana Underwood
Guest
October 10th : 2019

As we approach a new day, a new dawn, we lie praying in blood
and waiting with tears in our eyes. Every second we become less
like the person we once were.
Welcome to the new world.

This is the Zombie Apocalypse.

#292
Zombie Hunter
Member
October 10th : 2019

Do not punch a zombie or set fire to a zombie you will be wasting your time and putting yourself at risk.

Nothing kills these beasts except destroying the brain.

Remember this guy's n' Galls!

#293
Zombie Hunter
Member
October 10th : 2019

There is a video a sniper taking random people out, from the top of a building, another of a gang dragging humans who don't look infected behind their cars on rope people are right the main threat here is no law in place!

#294
Reece
Member
October 10th : 2019

I don't know how long this site is going to be up but I don't predict long. I have heard that it is spreading fast all over the world.

There are so many stories that I don't know what to believe like most people at the moment. I have spent most of the morning at the police station, we couldn't get inside butt police told me and everyone else to just get inside our homes and await further instruction.

#295
Pepper Max
Member
Moderator
October 10th : 2019

The numbers are ridiculous some sites say 984000 suspected cases and 90000 deaths!

I don't know what to believe as there are no official sites up or anyone giving the real facts!

#296
Reece
Member
October 10th : 2019

Everyone's wearing masks. If you don't have one of the standards dust masks they started to hand out then use something else.

People are using scarves bandanas or even clothing tied around their faces to prevent infection. Nothing appears to be able to prevent a bite from one of them. Once you've been bitten you'll turn into one of them.

#297
GerryRaf
Member
October 10th : 2019

Over the past few years there have been reports and accounts of cannibalism spread out from Miami to China. I'm scared this is caused by brain parasites.

#298
Zombie Hunter
Member
October 10th : 2019

@GerryRaf
"Brain parasites" it might be caused by the brain dead people in charge!
You can't strangle them, you have to make sure that the brain is destroyed or they keep coming at you.

#299
Reece
Member
October 10th : 2019

No one knows why they constantly crave human flesh.

#300
James TK
Member
October 10th : 2019

two of them are at my front door throwing themselves against it
i've boarded it up but i'm scared shitless!
we've turned the lights out and we've locked ourselves in the
bathroom waiting for help

#301
Reece
Member
October 10th : 2019

Fight then or defend yourself! Don't wait in there, they might
break it in, can't you get into your loft?
The flesh eaters are multiplying so quickly, I have never seen
anything like this in my life!
We are staying inside our offices here in central London. There's
no way we can go outside but we've made a report on the Police
website so hopefully they'll come soon.

#302
James TK
Member
October 10th : 2019

We are getting in the loft taking supplies of food and drink.
Cheers.

#303
ZombieSlayer
Member
October 10th : 2019

Cover your eyes, nose and mouth as best you possibly can. I'm wearing goggles and a dust mask.

#304
Reece
Member
October 10th : 2019

I've started to try and find weapons from the house and shed. I have garden pitch forks, knives and a baseball bat and I'm keeping them close at hand. I'm prepared for any invaders to my house, it's scary but it's strange I think I'm growing more confident the more I prepare.

#305
Beloti
Member
October 10th : 2019

Looking back at the news over the past week there were passengers on board a flight from Cairo that had to be restrained and received medical attention. There were also reports of cannibalism like attacks in Pakistan and even 10 cases of deaths in the past week from Swine Flu in the UK alone!

#306
ZombieSlayer
Member
October 10th : 2019

Be careful travelling in the dark, I have infra-red goggles but I'm a long term prepper so most people won't have them so just avoid travelling in the dark.
Be careful outhere guys!

#307
RyanC1
Guest
October 10th : 2019

There were also more than 30 reported cases of necrotizing fasciitis over the previous week (before this only around 15 cases had ever been reported). This flesh eating disease is rare and what's even stranger is that the 30 cases reported last week were all from areas with un-sanitized water!
This is crazy!

#308
Reece
Member
October 10th : 2019

The flesh eating zombies will stop at nothing to get to your flesh. Cover yourself up with duct tape and leather if you have it to make it harder for them to get to your skin.

Beware The number of looters and gangs is rising rapidly!

#309
Prepper Max
Member
Moderator
October 10th : 2019

Just watched video online!
I saw one of them being rammed by a car, the whole of the bottom half of his body was missing but he was still crawling and dragging his body along the ground.

#310
CarlyBenner
Guest
October 10th : 2019

The Army seems to be shooting randomly, trying to control the infection. I can see them from my apartment window, this is messed up. I know there are still civilians down there. I have video evidence of this!

#311
Zombie Hunter
Member
October 10th : 2019

The Top Ten worst places to try to survive the zombie apocalypse.

Cities

A shopping Mall
A Hospital
Pubs or Bars
A school
Police Stations
A traffic Jam
Apartments/Houses
High rise buildings
A graveyard

#312
Prepper Max
Member
Moderator
October 10th : 2019

Kit yourself out with the right clothing and weapons.

Think!!!

Water
Food
Defence
Shelter
Fire

These will save your life!
In any situation!

Think survival at all times!

 # 313
Steve E
Member
October 10th : 2019

It's crazy out there, its mayhem. I have never witnessed anything like this in my life. This is so horrible. I'm terrified, and we are in our home here in Utah.

#314
Mariaz33
Guest
October 10th : 2019

Please Keep Calm was the last thing a police officer said to us as we were running from the city here in France, are they really being serious or what? I'm staying with my aunt quite away from the city, we are making the house secure, though we have already had bricks thrown at the windows from looters.

 # 315
Everyoneisdead
Member
October 10th : 2019

im alone now everyone is dead what are we supposed to do just hide wait to be bitten infected or even worse raped by the sick and twisted looters i had to witness this happening to my cousin sarah who was only 13 i watched from under the bed as they terrorized then shot her just for fun and because they could there is no law here anymore.

#316
Johnny Smith
Guest
October 10th : 2019

I don't want to die!
I hope help comes soon!

#317
Steve E
Member
October 10th : 2019

It seems that you are safer staying inside with the windows and doors boarded up, keep weapons on you at all times.
We've been in all day and there's no sign of any help coming but at least we haven't contracted the virus or been victims of looting.
The dead are outside walking aimlessly around.

#318
Reece
Member
October 10th : 2019

Is anyone planning for long term survival? There doesn't seem to be much of a mention about that.

#319
Jessica
Member
October 10th : 2019

There are so many gangs all over the place looting and causing havoc, they make the zombie virus look less threatening! I'm so scared for my safety.

#320
Anthony
Member
October 10th : 2019

Is murder legal now?
I have just seen my neighbor three doors down being stabbed and robbed of his belongings. they were stamping on his head until it was just matter!

#321
Felicity
Member
October 10th : 2019

We are hiding out in our loft here in the U.S, we have food, drink and weapons up here and a tiny window, and it seems like the safest place to be at the moment.

#322
Caitlin
Member
October 10th : 2019

Keep down, keep out of sight and keep on moving. This is what I have been advised to do by one of the soldiers.
I went back inside bugger that, surely we are safer inside?

#323
Kevin
Member
October 10th : 2019

ISOLATION CAMPS IN OPERATION ACROSS THE GLOBE!

One isolation camp in the U.S has been breached and hundreds of the infected have escaped.

#324
Gary
Member
October 10th : 2019

Every patient with rabies will have hydrophobia, they foam at the mouth and it will be painful for them to swallow.
Whether this virus is connected to rabies or not I don't know but I'm heading out, right out to sea. Surely the ocean is the only safe place out there, but you'll need lots of food and water supplies. Just don't use your flare-gun!

#325
Alex K
Member
October 10th : 2019

You have to be bitten, scratched or exchange bodily fluids with an infected person to contract rabies. I think you have a point. Rabies doesn't normally transmit easily and isn't airborne, though I suppose if the virus has mutated it could transfer through the air.

#326
Ewan Mc
Member
October 10th : 2019

No one has immunity to the virus; it will attack anyone it comes into contact with.

#327
Figtinator
Member
October 10th : 2019

There are so many diseases that have spread from animals; all it would take would be for one human to become infected from a bite. This sounds like a mutation of rabies.

#328
Zombie slayer
Member
October 10th : 2019

Head for high ground, get to the top of a building, make it as hard as you possibly can for the zombies to get at you.

Stay Safe! Keep your eyes peeled.

#329
Paige
Member
October 10th : 2019

It's now time to start praying, I have already started.

#330
Zombie Slayer
Member
October 10th : 2019

The infected are attracted to light and movement, keep out of sight, turn off lights and keep quiet. If they can see you, then they won't stop until they get to you.

#331
Zombie Hunter
Member
October 10th : 2019

Get a gun or at the very least a melee weapon to protect you from both the infected and the looters. Always have a back-up weapon on you just in case. Make it as difficult as you can for the infected or looters to get into your home or base, set up traps if you can!

#332
Maxtor
Member
October 10th : 2019

Rabies affects all mammals including sea mammals. Suppose a whale or other sea mammal gets infected, suppose you drank from the water.
Just saying!

#333
Sarah Smith
Member
October 10th : 2019

Tom,
It's me Sarah Smith; I'm at home waiting for you. I can't get through on the phone or get any response from you or your family. I know this is clutching at straws but I'm worried sick.
I'm safe, I'm with our neighbours, Ted and his wife, and we have

boarded and secured the house as best we can.

I love you

Come home soon.

#334

Wayne D

Member

October 10th : 2019

There were online reports of a mystery flesh-eating illness in the Philippines only 3 months ago but no one has even mentioned this, not even online!

#335

Jayne P

Member

October 10th : 2019

Swine Flu returned recently in the USA, USSR and the UK only a few months ago, it didn't seem to hit the headlines though! It has to be connected in some way, it's over 5 years ago now that Swine Flu first hit the headlines, it may have mutated who knows with rabies like virus and this is the result.

#336

And a Vicar 1

Member

October 10th : 2019

All over the internet it's saying that the infected zombie-like beings have large blisters to the skin, pronounced veins and eyes which are completely blood-shot.

Is it legal to kill them? Even the ones who are in a zombie state, what if they find a cure? Does that make us murderers?

#337
Jayne P
Member
October 10th : 2019

If a virus like Rabies mutated with the Flu virus it could be transmitted through the air from coughing and sneezing as well as scratches and bites. Just think how quickly this could spread.

#338
Robert Foster
Member
October 10th : 2019

In 2013 virologists were preparing for a deadly bird flu mutation. The internet at the time was on meltdown, people were getting worried but it all seemed to just die down.

The deadly H7N9 bird flu could have been the cause of this in some strange mutated way.

I am just trying to make some sense of this to be honest. I think the government knew it was coming a long time ago, they knew they could not control it. I bet everyone in power is safe and warm and in no danger, with good food and sipping champagne about now.

While we just wait and die.

#339
Mikey2
Guest
October 10th : 2019

Virologists are now trying to make an antidote that was the last thing I saw on the online news website. They are only broadcasting old news on the news channels now, I bet they are all safe in there made up forts and secure silos by now.

#340
Robert Foster
Member
October 10th : 2019

Over 110 people in China were confirmed to be infected with H7N9, with well over 23 deaths, in 2013 alone from H7N9. These cases were located in China and Taiwan.

#341
Zombie Slayer
Member
October 10th : 2019

Always ask yourself questions when preparing to travel!

Where will you live?
What will you eat?
Where is your closest source of water?
Where will you head?

Ask yourself these questions, think about it and answer them first. There is no point ending up in a cabin in the sticks with hundreds of the infected outside while you are starving to death inside.

Be practical.

#342
Zombie Slayer
Member
October 10th : 2019

Protect your limbs at all times.

The infected don't need limbs to function but you will, they will not lose blood and die but you will unless you protect yourself.

#343
Zombie Slayer
Member
October 10th : 2019

Stockpile or find and take with you:

Flour

Water

Salt

Batteries

All things that you can later barter with. The dollar, the pound, it all is worthless now. Gold coins, food, water and weaponry will be the new currency.

People will be trading in their friends and family soon!

The infected won't be the only cannibals. When you're starving to death, how good does a cooked human leg sound? We are apex predators, we will do what we have to do to survive.

Think about it, every one of you are walking food to the infected and the survivors within the foreseeable future. I will not die with an onion shoved up my arise and a carrot in my mouth, that's for sure.

#344
Zombie Hunter
Member
October 10th : 2019

Think 3.
This will save your life knowing just how long you can live without air, water and food.
You can last approximately 3 minutes without air, 3 days without water and up to 3 weeks without food. Remember the 3's and use them as a guideline.
Good luck everyone. keep fighting them. I have to deal with some pricks at the back door. looters seem more of a problem than the infected.

#345
Radio
Member
October 10th : 2019

There are rumours that the government and the military will be using a form of Broadband HSMM a high speed, self-discovering, configuring, wireless computer network. This can literally run for days even from something as simple as a car battery.
This had been documented online over the last few years saying that radio operators in the US had created a wireless high speed data network.

#346
SkylerJ
Guest
October 10th : 2019

My brother recently returned from a business trip to Cairo. He was fine, nothing wrong with him. Then 10 days after he returned, he broke out with a high fever and flu like symptoms. He was taken to the hospital yesterday and basically put in quarantine as there were complications. I can't get near the hospital. The whole place is a war zone, with looters and the infected out in force here in Wyoming.

#347
Scared Shitless
Member
October 10th : 2019

This is it, this is the end. I cannot live in fear of getting eaten alive or worse (if you could possibly imagine). The looters are sick and twisted, I have witnessed then holding people prisoner. They had one man up on a cross naked; they were taking it in turns to shoot him, but slowly, in the hands and feet. It was a game to them, live target practice.

I only have one bullet as I killed as many of the infected as I could, it was a shame it couldn't have been those evil sadistic bastards instead. This seems the easiest and safest option, I don't want to roam around in an empty soulless shell or be used as a play thing, and this one bullet is a god send. I hope it's better on the other side.

#348
Radio
Member
October 10th : 2019

The National Guard, Armies all over and other military groups are being overrun. They can't control the spread of the infection. This was from a pirate radio source.

#349
Tony
Member
October 10th : 2019

On the news it is warning everyone to stay indoors. What I don't get is why some specific areas are being evacuated, and people not even allowed into their own streets. These people have to go with the army to the pop up bases and medical centres which I have seen some footage of online from all over the world. This does in no way seem fair, am I the lucky one?

I am at home with my Wife as secure as we can be for the time being while my friend is in a camp with the army, only time will tell I think which is safer.

Why the hell did they not have better plans? in place!

#350
Reece
Member
October 10th : 2019

There are so many videos online there are more videos of people trying desperately to get into boats. There was one from Brighton where everyone and his dog tried to get into the boats at the marina nearly every boat toppled over it was total devastation. Only a few got out safely people's heads were being trampled on, I never really liked the police before, but damn do I miss them now.

#351
Jayne P
Member
October 10th : 2019

We've just finished boarding up all of the windows and doors making the place secure, dad even put barbed wire and broken glass around the window ledges. We moved all of the ladders and garden tools from the shed in with us. It's so dark in the house now it's difficult to tell the difference between day and night. I spend all my time trying to get more information from the radio, there are no announcements yet just websites teaching you how to kill them Aim for the head, destroy the brain and don't get scratched or bitten.

There doesn't seem to be any fresh information, I can't watch any of the videos online, they're sick! I don't know what's in the content itself but reading the comments underneath I don't want to.

Will the infected decompose eventually?

#352
Zombie Hunter
Member
October 10th : 2019

Yes they will, but it would take at least a few years at a guess! So this will not help us immediately. I hope we can survive this. I'm doing my best; I've killed twenty-seven of the infected and counting! I hope the number will be a lot more by the end of the day.

#353
Jayne P
Member
October 10th : 2019

There are reports from a radio broadcast, saying that people who are dying naturally from natural causes are returning as Infected zombies, is this true? Do you know of any cases?

#354
Zombie Hunter
Member
October 10th : 2019

This happened to my father. We all assumed that he was initially infected and that the virus was lying dormant, but after hearing this it makes you think.

#355
Radio
Member
October 10th : 2019

On the pirate radio station I'm listening to it is reported from an unknown source that the (MERS) virus has mutated with the rabies virus. How much of this is true, I don't know. So what about the mystery flyer? I think it could be fake spam flyer going around to be honest!! I'm just reporting what I have heard.

#356
I Hate Gov
Member
October 10th : 2019

The Government are bastards they could have stopped this they are responsible for the death of my family and my friends thank you for ruining my life I'm so glad I worked my tits off every day paying taxes and jumping through hoops just to be a part of the rat race we were never going to win.
This no name virus they may as well call it the zombie virus. Will be the end? The great death of civilization (as we know it)?

#357
Andrea
Member
October 10th : 2019

Blood covered pavements outside our front door.
Where once stood people there are no more.
The world is a wasteland and we cannot escape.
 Murder, blood, death and rape.
Blood splatter warm, flowing, oozing, stained, sticky, and red.
Nothing disguises the smell of the dead.
So much blood, so little life, so little time.
Every second may be our last.
Blood rabid biters, evil zombie beings, rising from the dead.
Blood coursing, pumping blood, life, giving blood, now takes life

away.
Are we the ones who will rot and decay?
I want to survive.
To live another day.

#358
Jayne P
Member
October 10th : 2019

The post/poem above by Andrea was really good it's how we all feel.

#359
Ron P
Member
October 10th : 2019

It's everyone, man, women and even child for himself out there! We're lucky to be in though I'm scared being in a block of flats. My wife is worried some groups will set the whole building on fire. Something needs to be done it's not just the infected that are out of control.

#360
Michael566
Member
October 10th : 2019

I'm out in the deep south, there is no one for miles, and we have always been self-sufficient.

I will protect my family until my dying last breath with as much force as is needed.

#361
Reece
Member
October 10th : 2019

Same here, respect to you Michael566.We all need to be thinking of the self-sufficient route at the moment and for the future in order to survive.

#362
Caitlin
Member
October 10th : 2019

With the infrastructure collapse that we are seeing and with no policing how much longer could we survive anyway?
The high number of looters easily outnumber regular survivors or even the infected!

#363
Dixon17
Member
October 10th : 2019

No, trust me there is more of the walking undead outside our building. There are hundreds and I mean hundreds of them. We are up high but God help us if they get in here.

#364
MerpLol
Member
October 10th : 2019

I'm going now to my bunker in the garden to wait this out– well I's an old world war two shelter that I kept as it was my grand-mothers property and we used to play there as kids!
My family thought I was crazy before but now everyone's here and begging me to take them or their children. There are twelve of us going in a three person bunker the space is bad enough but I had prepared it with enough food, water etc. for three people.

#365
Reece
Member
October 10th : 2019

I don't see animals attacking us well no more than usual. They don't seem infected I have a vision of towns and cities being overrun by animals hopefully they can finish off these zombie bastards.

#366
Kevin
Member
October 10th : 2019

I killed someone today I never thought I would be writing that or saying it!. It was a lady, well a shell of a lady she went to bite my daughter so I used the baseball bat I had as a weapon. Whatever anyone tells you is bullshit, it's so hard to kill them they keep coming for you and trying to get to your flesh until their brains are a pile of mush.

#367
Help us now!
Member
October 10th : 2019

Please help Us!!!!!
There are eight of us; we are on the London eye in central London.
There are three women, four men and one child Including myself. The London Eye is at a standstill, we can see people running around being attacked by other people. They look as if they are rabid, biting one another.
The sky is filled with smoke and we can see fires across the whole of London and cars crashing into one another. There is a bus on its side, children as young as five holding their teddy bears running covered in blood.
There was a police presence earlier on but now I have seen nothing, we have been up here for five hours and we're feeling sick and dizzy. It feels like the air is running out, we are all sitting on the floor and trying to calm one another. We have tried to make contact with other people in other cages on the London eye, but no one knows what is going on. We have no internet connection and none of our phones are sending anything, I'm writing this and I will keep pressing send in hope. Wade said he had a connection for a few seconds but it's gone now. We have a diabetic on board and we need help now! We only have an oat snack bar, can of coke and a pack of peppermints between all of us. We have to pee in bottles which are virtually impossible for

the ladies, though all of us have lost our dignity by now. We need urgent help now, get here now!

#368
Zombie Hunter
Member
October 10th : 2019

I have copied and posted your request for help on to the police form website. To be honest it doesn't look good, that form was obviously set up to give hope. The emergency telephone numbers are down as are all the police stations, if they're not empty then a gang of looters will be in there. If I was you use whatever you have on you to carefully try to break the glass and get down, it's the only chance you have of survival.

Though you are in the safest possible place away from the infected and the looters food and water may be a slight problem.

#369
Help us now!
Member
October 10th : 2019

How the hell are we going to get down from here?
We will wait it out as long as we can we really have no other option.

#370
Zombie Slayer
Member
October 10th : 2019

The police website is no more!

Be prepared to kill your friends and family if they become infected. They will turn and come after you, they have no memories. This sounds terrible but the whole situation is messed up, you will have to if you want to survive. My advice is if you have symptoms end it before you turn or get someone else to end it for you.

#371
SupashopBristol
guest
October 10th : 2019

If the police/Army are reading this please hurry!

Timmy is ill We are all here and we've made friends with other survivors. Mr. Smith is looking after us, he's a good man.

We're hiding out at the top of the Supashop Store in Bristol it's cold and we're hungry and scared

Come quickly!

Please

#372
Reg
Member
October 10th : 2019

The sites are dropping so quick, the servers probably can't handle the traffic!

There are no police sites up to log incidents down as Z said!

Don't get captured by looters, there are so many gangs of looters. We saw one truck with around twenty people; hostages in the back tied up, all we could hear was blood curdling screams.

They're collecting their future food supplies.
There are some fucked out crazies out in force!

#373
Zombie Slayer
Member
October 10th : 2019

Where there is one zombie there will more than likely be others.
I have just found this out, we saw one, killed it and thought we
were fine until around twenty more came out of the woods We
got the hell out of there quickly, you can out-run them if there are
only a few.

#374
Caitlin
Member
October 10th : 2019

I did leave after all.
I'm safe now, I'm at an Army base but we are not allowed
phones. I am in a queue they take your phones and all of your
belongings. Then you are sent to quarantine and have tests, it's
really scary but this might be my only hope of survival.
I have a vision of us all being shipped off to an island that is safe
and starting a fresh, I don't really know what the future holds
but it must be better than this.
There are so many people here it is total mayhem, I feel as if I'm
in safe hands now and in the best possible place.

#375
Zombie Slayer
Member
October 10th : 2019

@Caitlin
GET THE HELL OUT OF THERE, THE CAMPS ARE LIKE
TRAPS TRYING TO CONTROL THE INFECTION BY KILLING
THE HEALTY PLEASE JUST GET AS FAR AWAY GTOM THERE
AS POSSIBLE THE CAMPS ARE NOT SAFE DO NOT TRUST
ANYONE!

Try to keep your distance from the undead. They will try to grab
you, they will try to scratch and infect you, and they will
definitely try to eat your flesh and brains.

#376
Reece
Member
October 10th : 2019

The end is nigh!
If you have the virus its game over simple as that. There is no
vaccine or cure to end this madness.

#377
Megan x
Member
October 10th : 2019

There's footage online now of three army bases being overrun by the infected here in England! No one can regain control!!

Nowhere is safe, I would get away from the army and the bases there will be too many people there. No wonder they are being over-thrown by the infected. Get the hell out of there!

#378
Zombie Slayer
Member
October 10th : 2019

The infected deads eye sight seems to be hazy, they can only see you from about fifteen feet away, it might just be me but this seems to be true.

I'm having problems with my internet connection, it keeps going on and off, and many websites all over are down including the big ones.

#379
Discard
Guest
October 10th : 2019

This site was down a few minutes ago, it said temporary unavailable.

Glad it's back up now.

Whatever caused this a Flu/Ebola/Rabies man made or just a mutation matters not now! The end result that the dead are walking and they are hungry for our flesh the ones who are left have or are going completely stir crazy there is no law in place murder is legal now! I'm scared I have never been afraid or had these feelings in my lifetime and I'm no pussy!

#380
Carnage2014
Member
October 10th : 2019

"Bring out your dead"
This is the new plague.
What is the next step, do we put crosses on our doors if any of us infected?
Why the hell are the authorities just not helping at all?
There is no law here, just rioting and flesh eaters.

#381
Carothium
Member
October 10th : 2019

A lot of people are finding the power is going out in certain countries.
There seems to be less of a military presence now, but more screams and gangs of looters chanting! I haven't seen an aircraft for over an hour now which is kind of worrying.

#382
Ruth B
Member
October 10th : 2019

This is the new Black Death!
I don't want to die!

I had a message from a relative in Hawaii saying that the virus spread so quick there because they are om a small island and have millions of residents it was total carnage there everyone was trying to get of the island my cousin was at the police station the last time I spoke to her she said they were filling the police sells up with healthy people! It seems like a good idea to me.

No one can believe how quick this virus has spread, though I can see from reports online that there were cases of a mystery virus and an array of cannibalistic reports late last night!

#383
Zombie Slayer
Member
October 11th : 2019

"We are all carrying the virus, every single one of us."

Nothing could have prepared me for this, I thought the infected ones were the zombies and if we kept away and stayed safe (sticking to the rules and not getting the infection) we could maybe make it out alive. I feel sick now, I didn't before but I keep feeling hot then cold as if I might turn into one of them.

Who knows what effects it could cause on the body, everyone's different and I thought you only turned if you got infected, bitten, scratched or got their blood or even saliva near yours. I was wrong, all of us were wrong. Today I watched an old man die, he had a heart attack. He couldn't face killing his wife who had recently turned from a bite and he died from shock. He died and came back as one of them.

I didn't realise (like most of the group) that we were all carrying the virus; we spoke openly about it today. Three members of the group assumed it was common knowledge and even said that they were told when they escaped from a camp at the army base. This changed everything, who knows what the virus is doing inside of us right now!

Who knows what changes are taking place now, will it destroy us from within?

Take our life from us when it chooses to.

Its early days there is no point asking questions none of us have answers to.

Are we all dead already?

Are we the walking dead?

Are we just walking cadavers?

The only difference now between us is that we don't hunt for human flesh or exist solely to spread the virus.

I lost faith and hope today; does anyone actually want to live in a world with this virus controlling us, calling the shots?

The world would not be a place I would like to live in.

At best if the zombie epidemic was over we would have a life on meds to control it. I don't want to live in a world like this.

Death note

#384

James M

Member

October 11th : 2019

There is no such thing as great death or a beautiful death, just an end to everything we know, and everything we have seen through our eyes and listened to.

Blood stained, soiled clothes, lying on a rotting corpse waiting to be devoured.

An end to dignity, an end to what might have been.

We will never know if we will turn and become one of them unless we destroy our own brains first, but what is worse!

Is there a heaven or hell?

Only time will tell.

James Marich
Only 17 years and 2 days on this earth. October 11th 2019

#385
RidleyP
Member
October 11th : 2019

Is anyone still online?

#386
Mariah66
Member
October 11th : 2019

If we are all carrying the virus it's …
GAME OVER.
@RidleyP
Yep just about, going really quite online now!
Most sites are down and hard to keep my connection it keeps dropping in the US here!

Unable to connect to the server!
If problems persist please contact the website administrator.

Loading Error

404 PAGE NOT FOUND!

#387
RidleyP
Member
October 11th : 2019

I too believe that we are all carrying the virus, for these effects to take place so quick!
I PM'd a few people but have got nothing back!
Any Updates Prepper Max?

#388
RidleyP
Member
October 11th : 2019

Anyone!!!!!

Hold on there is trouble/noises outside!

#389
Carothium
Member
October 11th : 2019

I'm still here,
The gangs/groups/terrorists whatever you call them are chanting and singing shouting waving flags shooting their guns at anything that moves and setting fire to every building, We are so worried they are coming this way!

#390
Carothium
Member
October 11th : 2019

I now officially believe in God.

"Please God Help us all"!

#391
Carothium
Member
October 10th : 2019

Anyone out there?

Found Journal in Camden, London, England

It's a turf war out there. There are gangs of survivors fighting each other for safety, shelter, food and water. Gangs of youths are fighting the frail and elderly for their supplies. They're looting, destroying and blowing up buildings just for fun!

The dead are walking, attacking, eating and feasting on the closest flesh to them. They have no preference, they just want to feast. Once bitten the infection spreads rapidly, they are producing more of their own kind at a rate which is making this outbreak look unstoppable. When it first began the problem was limited to the infected but now it's everywhere, it's everyone, no one is safe anymore.

The sad fact is that it is every man, woman and child for themselves. I've just witnessed a mother killing another human being just for some milk that was left in the supermarket. She battered a woman's head in, she didn't stop kicking until the woman was lifeless. I also saw a boy of around nine years old stab a man for a packet of cigarettes (of all things)! Where is this going to end? I've seen innocent passers-by desperately seeking safety only be doused with gasoline and set on fire purely for entertainment. There's nothing I could have done to help, I would have wound up becoming just another victim of their cruel games.

You can't let your guard down for a minute, you are never safe. The infected come at you both day and night. They don't appear to sleep, they just keep moving, desperately seeking flesh.

They don't seem to be able to see in the dark any more than we can (we can use this to our advantage whenever possible). They crave human flesh, they are constantly rotting and decaying by the minute.

The infected have no memories, if your husband turned in front of your eyes he wouldn't even blink before devouring your brain and flesh. When a loved one or a friend dies – they are dead, they are not what they appear on the outside. When you get bitten you have a few moments or minutes when you appear to be dead. You have no pulse but you jolt back to life as if you have been given a defibrillator to the heart. The eyes are different and general appearance. I have seen them roam – some alone and some in groups and some seem to move much faster than others. I have seen the infected attracted by noise. They all seem to have the same symptoms (give or take a few) but there does seem to be varying times from a person dying to their corpse reanimating. The strength of the infected seems to be that of the host, if the person was a body builder, he would have that same strength, though all of them just go crazy clawing, scratching and biting to get human flesh. They do this with intent and have the same rush of endorphins as we would in a fight or flight situation, although there is no flight for them, only fight.

I have even witnessed someone after they got bitten who seemed to have a fit. They did not change at all. They were devoured within ten minutes by zombies but showed no signs of coming back to life after the bite.

There is only one way of killing them, destroying the brain. Nothing, I repeat, nothing else will work. I have tried everything, and I mean everything! No body blows, wounds or shots will do anything apart from maybe slow them down. I find using something sharp like an axe and attacking them on the back of the head works like a charm, though you do have some trouble removing the axe sometimes. They do not fight each other but they do bang into one another and fall over one another's feet.

They cannot speak, they moan and groan but this seems to only occur when they have their sights on something they intend to feast on, a target.

They show no ability to hold onto items (you don't see them walking down the street with a mobile phone or carrying a bag full of flesh) though they do use their hands for attacking and to assist them whilst eating.

If you cut off their legs or arms they will still slide, crawl or shuffle. They don't die from loss of blood and they do not need a heart for the brain to remain active. You can become infected by being bitten, scratched or having immediate contact with their blood or saliva.

When fighting you need to keep your mouth covered or closed and be careful that nothing gets into your eyes or open wounds (I wear glasses and have wiped away many blood smears from my glasses) I look after them, a new pair could be hard to come by.

I can't say that I've found a best or safe place to go but I stay away from crowds and noise. I generally don't stay in one place for too long.

It seems like this has been going on for a lot longer than it actually has. I am going to move out of the city now that I know my family have gone, the ones that made it out alive. Watching some of your family turn is something you can't come back from.

If I don't end up being infected, I'll probably get murdered by these gangs of vigilantes, the gang numbers get bigger by the day. Food here is scarcer than ever and I have forgotten what clean water tastes like, though I yearn for it. I'm moving on.

Medications are the hardest things to get. They were the first things everyone started to store. The first shop I saw looted was a large medical chain. At first there was a strange comradery, people would throw you goods, say, do you fancy this, even if they did not know you. Now they would kill you soon as look at you.

I have heard there are bartering trade centres all over the city but there are stories of people never returning. I would not entertain it for anything.

People are killed for their coats, shoes, trainers and gold teeth. Everything is worth something to someone. What are the rules now? None I guess. I never thought it would take the government this long to restore order. I imagine a large, American, helicopter coming in and saving us all. Sleep is the luxury I look forward to the most. I'm headed for the country as this city is filled with broken glass, ash, body parts and decay.

I pray for everyone.

These blood-filled streets show no sign of hope.

Diary account found in Chelmsford, Essex.

I am alone, I don't think I have ever felt so alone in my life, I don't have a partner a wife or even a best friend apart from my dog Rocky, they say that a dog is man's best friend this is so true Rocky died yesterday I am so gutted! I have a sinking feeling inside my stomach I am truly lost, dogs are amazing they are lovely they cuddle you when you are feeling blue, play and even want the leftovers you don't wont.

Rocky went outside to go on his usual routine to the toilet in the garden, he limped back to me covered in blood, he had been bitten by one of them, I shot the thing in the head with my air rifle, it took over twenty shots and a baseball to the head a few times to finish the job off properly and about an hour to get the blood off.

I humanely put an end to Rocky's life and buried him in the garden, I shot him in the head, maybe it was not the right thing to do but I did not want him to suffer, starving like we were together, I will never take away the image from my head it was awful, his big eyes looking back at me with such trust and just love.

I am in my late thirties, we have had the internet now for over 13 years, I lived with my parents for as long as I can remember, it was easier it was safe it was all I knew, they both passed away a few years back, mum and dad were both ill, mum was an alcoholic, time wasn't on her side, dad passing on just sealed the deal, I was a carer and a son but whatever they were I loved them to bits, I miss them both today as much as I did when they went birthdays and Christmastime are the worst.

I was an internet addict, it kind of crept up on me and took over my life really, I have online friends but they are gone now with the internet down, I used to do online food shopping and buy everything I need online it is the way of the world now more shops are disappearing by the minute, I think I was one of the first to realize something was wrong, looking through endless internet boards, I looked at patterns and news using my own form of big data I work in domain names and websites buying and selling them online for a profit I was not lucky enough to be there in the initial dot com boom, but I was waiting for the next big thing, I suppose I earned a fair portion of online real-estate, the focus for me was always money when my mum and dad went I had enough money in the safe to buy a flash pad in Chelsea, to buy a little house in the country, after I had the money and bought all the essentials as you do my cupboard has thirty bags of sugar, and twenty jars of powdered milk and enough toilet roll that would last me a year.

I hated buying and going out daily or running out of all the essentials, it was a waste of time and effort, My neighbour Mr. Jonas was kind of a friend, we used to have tea and cake and chat for a while once a week at least, it was a bit of physical company for both of us (neither of us really liked each other but we used to tolerate one another and have a weekly rant putting the world to rights), it served as a kind of therapy for both of us. I haven't seen Mr. Jonas since the morning the infection broke out, I found his car a few blocks from our maisonette, his car seat was covered in blood, and I suppose I have no other option than too fear the worst.

When I saw his car I ran straight back inside and collected my belongings, the police were ordering people to get away from the city. I travelled by foot and spent some days and nights sleeping rough until I found myself in the middle of nowhere. I think somewhere along the line I had lost track of time, I didn't carry a watch with me and my phone was down.

I saw an old abandoned house in a field which looked as if it had been taken straight from the pages of a fairy tale book, it was deceiving because it was far from a fairy tale inside! The house was a mess and it stank to high heaven, though to my surprise there was somebody living there. The old man who occupied the house was kind enough to take me in, he was oblivious to the events unfolding, he hadn't seen the news or even read a paper or listened to the radio, for entertainment he would spin his old 78 records he was skinny mainly skin and bones and had a beard that was tangled or matted hanging down with some leftover food still attached.

I walked into the living room and he offered to make me a hot beverage, I could see he was struggling so I made it for him, the once white mug was now dark and stained but hygiene wasn't high on my list of priorities right now. I poured myself and the elderly man a hot and sugary cup of tea it was the best cup of tea that I had ever had.

He offered me a room for the night, it had formerly been his daughter's bedroom, and it was filled with posters from the nineteen seventies and a lot of pink! I slept like a log after listening to the old man's stories about how his wife had died in some strange farming accident and how his daughter was some big shot lawyer deep in the heart of the city but only ever came to see him at Christmas but hadn't even seen him for the past few years. The old man showed me some letters that he had written to his daughter, there must have been over fifty of them all sealed and with stamps on them, just her name was written on the envelopes as he had no address and he told me that he wondered if her name was even the same now as she may have married. It was sad that all that was going through my mind was that he must have done something terrible in the past not only to be living like he was but for nobody to care, he was kind of just waiting to die and the saddest thing was that it somewhat resembled my life. I didn't want this as my future, as I lay on the hard wooden bed I promised myself that I would want for a better future and that maybe I would look for a partner later on.

The next morning as I walked down the stairs I noticed the few wooden, chipped and broken steps with holes in them, they didn't look safe to me. It was extra chilly downstairs, I noticed the fire was still roaring from the night before, then the door caught my eye, it was open and the old man was lying on the floor with his head propped to one side. I couldn't make him out properly, I rubbed my eyes. I thought I was seeing things at first but as I got closer the left side of his head was virtually non-existent, his brain had been eaten and his body resembled the remnants of a person who'd just jumped in front of a train. He was dead to say the least, there was a large trail of blood trailing out of the door, smeared across the floor it continued.

I was numb, I did not know what to do as I carried his body outside of the building and left it there. I scooped up the rest of the remains (nearly being sick the whole time). As I searched the place I found an old shot gun there were only two bullets left inside but no other ammo that I could find.

I left the house and continued to walk, after a while I saw a man but as I got closer I could tell it wasn't a man but an empty shell of a man coming straight for me. I fired a shot, it was a direct hit in the forehead he went down side wards I did not look at him again. I started walking back to the house but had not realized how far I had walked, I felt like I was in the middle of a real life computer game it was all so surreal. As I walked back two people came at me I did bother to try and talk to them, I knew they had been infected I could tell by the way they were walking. They were unsteady on their feet and kind of leaning over to one side, their hands raised with blood and saliva still dripping from their mouths. It suddenly struck me that I only had one bullet left, I zigzagged around them and got close enough to hit one of them in the back of the leg, he fell to the ground and I ran as fast as I could, more of them were appearing out of nowhere I think the gun firing had attracted them. As I approached the cottage there was a lady, she was infected she made a strange moaning noise and came at me, it all seemed to happen so quickly, I shot her, I missed her head but hit her in the shoulder, it startled her but she continued to come at me. I shoved her back and ran into the house, I locked the door behind me and checked all of the doors and windows inside to make sure they were all locked.

I looked outside, there must have been over twelve of them, that's when I stopped counting and I started to look for more ammunition. I ransacked the house and after thirty minutes or more I found a pack it was in the most obvious of places in the man's bedroom under some underwear next to a copy of the bible. I opened the front page it was supposed to be blank but written inside was the following:

"Can I be forgiven? I hope I can when there are people far worse than me out there.

I didn't choose to become this person it just happened, I don't blame anyone else but if I could do it all over again I would but I'd be very different, the choices and the actions we take either make or break us."

I continued to flick through the book there was large writing written with a fountain pen with letters to his wife and daughter as well as letters to God, it was more like a diary.

"Today I stopped drinking and I have faith that with your help I can do this"… it went on the book was almost full up but it was only written on one side of the page leaving the original text from the bible.

I threw the book on the floor, it felt wrong reading something so strange yet so personal, I replaced the used cartridges in the gun and filled all of my pockets with the bullets. I didn't want to be a sitting duck but was afraid of making a noise and attracting more of them. They were banging on the windows and doors, I boarded the windows up as best I could and started to reinforce the door using anything I could see. I drank another mug of tea and found a tin of cold beans, the taste was delicious, I pictured myself in the future stocking up on cold beans and being back in my flat, my so called bad life seemed perfect now. The day lasted forever and the moaning and groaning and the sound of their nails on the windows and doors was incessant. There was a hatch to the roof of the house, I got up there quietly, there were now over fifty of them all ages and sizes. Some looked worse than others, some had limbs removed and some looked like walking skeletons. I looked into the distance all around and realized just how isolated I was out here, in the distance was a town I could see lights but to walk it would take a good hour or so and it was just starting to get dark I didn't want to risk it. Days went by and I did not pluck up any more courage to go in search of help (if there was any).

I now officially hate cold beans and the water is starting to taste funny, cup a soups that have a use by date of over fifteen years old taste like you would expect them to! I continually built the fire up, it was so cold I was burning the furniture I could safely burn and the numbers of the dead were growing outside, it was like they were queuing especially for my flesh, just as if they were at a sale on Boxing Day. The same ones stayed at the front, I was amused by this, I wondered why the numbers were growing, and it must have been the smoke from the fire attracting them. I had no choice but to keep the fire going, it had started to snow it had no effect on them but it did me it must have got to below freezing. I could not stop shivering even with the fire on, I could not relax, I kept thinking this is it, how long could I survive in here? And even worse how long could I survive out there if I choose that path.

They told us to get out of major cities, but I would have been safer there than here. I'm all alone now with little or no chance of being rescued, I have never been a hero, more the underdog, and the wimp. I hate violence of any kind, I don't know what scares me more dying alone, dying in general or being eaten alive watching them feast on my flesh as I scream in horror, I can honestly say I can think of nothing worse.

I looked outside there was even more of them (or maybe it just seemed that way), I didn't look at them as people which was strange it was almost as if it they were rabid dogs all in a pack waiting to devour my flesh.

I had decided that whatever would go down they would not do it, they would not devour my flesh, whether I knew about it or not.

Now it was a matter of principle I grabbed some rocks, sticks and bits of wood, I threw them as far as I could into the trees and in the surrounding areas to try and distract them. It didn't work, some of them walked over to investigate but returned because of the moaning and banging. I waited until the next day, I took the boards from one of the biggest windows (it had been smashed and I didn't even realize it), as I took the board down they started to come in I fired one shot, then another, then another. I killed exactly ten of them then boarded the window back up (even squashing one of their hand inside) I tossed it into the fire. Ten down but so many more to go.

It was light now, I walked to the roof and with my gun I started shooting the ones that were the biggest threat to me. Most of them were country types with waistcoats and scarves still hanging from their battered bodies, one of them still had his glasses on and one had protective eyewear and three of them still wore green chunky wellington boots, this amused me it almost felt like a sketch from a comedy show. I started making names for them (it passed the time) I shot sue, I made up little stories about what she used to do for a living before all this happed. Sue was a traffic warden it wasn't hard to terminate her. Phil was a tax man (I hated paying tax) and Terry with his hoody and baseball cap covered in blood looked like a yob, I enjoyed getting rid of him the noise of them moaning was making me feel sick, I screamed out, I know it was wrong but after the gun shots I had fired who gave a shit really? I used the last bullet that I had on me, on Mr. fancily he was my old headmaster he was a bastard, he was greasy and balding just like the zombie though the zombie looked better until I blew his brains out! The residue of brains from the shot covered the others they kind of flinched it was funny though they never tried eating the dead rotting flesh of their own.

I felt quite honored that my flesh was special, ok I am a big lad, a bit of prime meat here maybe? Too much to eat in one go why not put some in the deepfreeze to last the winter? They don't seem to need to drink though I think I would have gone down well with a nice wine course (it would have to be an expensive one). The only trouble is do you go for white or red wine? I think white, as I thought about wine I really fancied some I was not a drinker but I craved it. I went on the lookout around the house for wine, I found about half a cup of sherry it looked like cooking sherry but it was close enough to wine and it was alcoholic. Next to the bottle was a cigar, it was quite small and it was wrapped, I lit it on the fire and started to talk like an English gentlemen of yesteryear this passed a few minutes. Looking out from the roof the numbers seemed to grow even more, I now was a sitting steak, I ran all over franticly thinking pacing up and down holding my chin thinking, then it came to me I was going to go for it.

I padded my neck up and wore the old man's beanie hat with some socks inside, I was not going to get bitten. I grabbed the gun and some petrol and started covering the house in petrol, this had to be done quickly. I opened the door with a burning homemade wick in hand, I threw this at the zombie then ran up to the loft. I threw the gun and jumped, I rolled and picked up the gun. My plan worked it cleared them, all the commotion attracted them, there were still a few, I took out two of them the cabin now started to go up in flames. I could feel the heat from where I was standing, I ran as fast as I could, it was dark, I kept running for a while then walked until it was light. I heard a noise as I sat under a tree, I turned around and one lunged for me, it scratched my hand as it was trying to latch on, I killed it then sat down. I felt OK but was worried about contracting the infection this way, as I write this I now feel worse I have a slight fever that is rising, I don't feel well, I think this is it! As I read a page from the bible then write this where the old man had stopped, I feel somewhat closer to religion and God than I have ever before. I can't write anymore I fell too ill I'm going to try and make it to the town nearby.

Notes Found in Cumbria, England

I'm not sure if this will help anyone but I will write down what I have learnt so far.

I used to be a police officer, but there's no law and no such thing as order now, so I may as well be wearing a traffic warden's uniform. In fact for my own safety, I've changed out of my uniform and back into my civi clothes. I've witnessed colleagues of mine kicked to death and left by the side of the road like a piece of meat. It wasn't even the zombies that did it. This was just rogue survivors, teenagers and people in their twenties; they seem to be enjoying the power and the lawlessness of it all. They've smashed windows, burnt out cars and shops and set fire to people without a thought, both to children and the elderly. There's just no stopping them. To be quite honest these guys are just as much of a threat as the infected. Maybe more – the infected don't move so fast and their behaviour is much more predictable. But neither of them have any emotion, feelings or conscience and neither show any signs of guilt or remorse. It's war, as gangs fight the infected, the gangs loot and they cause havoc everywhere and the infected are after everyone, spreading the infection and producing more of their own kind.

When the virus hit, the only problem was containing the infected but now...well now the problem is everywhere and everyone.

It's pure mayhem and nobody has any power, control or authority over them.

Please, if you are reading this, don't Trust Anyone! Don't let your guard down, not even for a millisecond because you may well pay for that mistake with your life.

The infected come both day and night but they don't seem to be able to see in the dark any better than us. Their bodies are deteriorating by the day, rotting, but it doesn't stop them. They seem to crave human flesh. They're dead, but they're not dead, they no longer have any human traits. Once a person is bitten they quickly deteriorate and die, seemingly coming back to life with a jolt, but they are no longer human at this point. Once turned their eyes become dead, they don't seem to have any memory, they just roam the streets craving flesh. They don't sleep (not ever) they just wander endlessly.

I have noticed that the rate at which people turn can vary from as much as a few minutes to a few hours. At this point in time I'm unsure as to why this is, but once turned these things seem to take on the strength of the body of its host.

We need to figure out some way to immunize ourselves against this thing. It's the only way. I witnessed a man, I would say he was in his late twenties, he'd been bitten, he started to fit, his body involuntarily jolting as it clashed with the concrete beneath him. But this time it seemed different. This man seemed to recover, although I didn't stay around long enough to find out what happened next. He and people just like him, could be the answer that everyone is so desperately searching for.

The only way of killing the infected is to totally (and I mean totally) destroy the brain. I find an axe to the head to be the most effective way to do this. The infected seem to travel together in a pack. I've never seen them fight each other and they seem to no longer have the ability to grasp things in their hands. They can't speak but just let out a continual gut wrenching groan. They are extremely resilient. I cut the leg from one of the infected with an axe. He fell to the floor but then used his hands to pull himself across the floor, and they just keep going until you get the brain.

You can become infected through the transfer of blood and

saliva, so it's advisable to cover your mouth and even your eyes if possible. I have seen people turn from this. I wear glasses which are constantly smeared with blood and other debris from killing these things but they work well to protect my eyes.

I can't tell you the best place to head to because nobody seems to know. I'm heading as far away from the city as possible as the numbers of the infected are sure to be fewer where it's not so densely populated. I'm writing this now as things are growing worse by the day now and I fear that if I manage to outwit the infected then death from fellow survivors will be inevitable. Food is becoming more and more scarce and medicines are rapidly dwindling. Batteries are now the biggest commodity. I would kill for a pack of painkillers and a change of shoes or even for a clean shave. There have been rumours that there is a certain place in London that people go to trade things but I have only heard horror stories about that place – about people that headed that way and were never seen again. People are being killed for such things as trainers, scarves and coats and old cell phones – that's how bad it's got! The streets are filled with bodies, blood, glass and ashes. The stench is almost unbearable. The lawlessness will be our downfall. The infection was just a spark to a long burning flame.

Stay safe, be aware and move away from the city while you still can!

Journal Found New York City. USA

October 2019

I don't think we'll ever truly know what caused this, though there have been rumours that it was some kind of mutation of bird flu but my theory is that the virus was manmade.

When the infection first broke the so called undead, the infected were everywhere.

My job before all this had started was as a freelance photographer and I had taken some photos of empty graves which I sold to the New York Times, eight photos at forty dollars each. The government started to dispose of bodies that were still buried, just in case! Thousands upon thousands of bodies were burnt; the smell of the decomposed bodies being burnt sent the air putrid.

For some reason no one took any notice, no one seemed bothered that graveyards were beginning to empty and rumours were everywhere that they were burning bodies!

No one knew why, this was too eerie not to be connected to the cause of the virus itself!

There had been reports of an unidentified virus killing people across the globe, the numbers were rapidly increasing. This mystery virus was taking the lives of people and spreading fear throughout the rest of us. According to the news reports it was the young and the elderly that were most at risk but no one was safe, the virus spread too quickly. The reports started as people behaving strangely, possessed almost by the devil some said, these beings were rampaging the streets of New York hungry for flesh. Social media went wild, there were reports of aliens, Jesus returning, the reckoning and the end of the world, people were barricading themselves in their houses, looting for supplies and attacking each other, all desperate to protect their families from this oncoming storm which was quickly devastating life as we knew it. When the phone lines went down, I realized that I was alone. Ok I was a lame photographer but I liked my life. I had been lucky enough to say goodbye to my mother and father before the technology died, a tearful video call but more than most, so I was grateful for that. We had reminisced about our holidays whilst tearfully trying to keep each other spirits up. Mum and Dad volunteered to go to quarantine with one of the government sectors, I wasn't sure at the time and didn't want to advise them as it could have meant the difference between life and death but when I think about it now I have a gut feeling that they're dead. People have told me that they had seen their families shot in front of them. I had hazy footage online shown to me of people being lined up against a wall and then being shot in their masses. There were posters all over town telling people not to go with the government because they would be killed. The phones and internet have just fizzled out. I decided to stay here in New York for the time being, if you squint it doesn't actually look much different than before, when the streets used to be filled with businessmen and women as well as vast amounts of tourists and drug dealers to prostitutes. These have been replaced with the walking dead, they creep and moan and crash into things whilst slowly pursuing flesh.

I haven't seen another living soul in weeks. At least I'm in my own apartment, who says women aren't tough? The man from across the hall, Mike was one of the most wonderful people I've ever had the privilege to call a friend. Mike my best friend. Mike lived just three steps across the hall. We were the only two people in the block. Mike was the owner of the florist shop downstairs, he had a partner named Josh and a dog Truffles, a funny looking little thing, and he was forever in and out of my apartment.

We all lived between the two apartments, blacking out the windows and boarding them up with wood. We even made up a sign which we put in the front window of the shop saying, property to let upstairs, to ensure that no one would suspect that we were in there. Just next to Mike's florist was the entrance to our apartments, it had a large solid wooden door with double locks and in front of that was a large metal framed gate which covered the door all the way to the top. It always used to feel like living in fort Knox but I was I glad of it now.

There was really only the one way in or out of the apartment, apart from out of Mike's bedroom window, where you climb out on a ledge which had a metal ladder to climb down. Mike went down to the shop to investigate a noise and to look for Josh but he never came back. Josh never came back either. I was left to look after Truffles, she ate better than me most nights, from steak to boiled fish.

The day Mike went downstairs and never returned must have been the worst so far, I counted over three hundred zombies walking past. Food is starting to run out now. I've only got two tins of beans left in the cupboard, and I'm not sure what I'll do when they run out. Though there are a few condiments left. I ate ketchup from a cereal bowl with a spoon last night, but it tasted better than it sounds, it was almost like a thick cold tomato soup.

The water stopped weeks ago, that hit me the hardest, me and Mike were lucky enough to raid a newsagents that was a few doors up, we managed to get some bottled water, cat and dog food and tinned food. It took us four trips to get the stuff back to the apartment, we assumed more people would sit it out, more loners like us but they didn't.

There was a strong military presence at the beginning, they were even banging at our gates and shouting to see if places were occupied. Mike had to lock the dog in the bathroom because it was barking like mad, they seemed to just do one sweep of the area, and they were shooting any zombies they came across. Part of me actually wanted to go out and go with the military, but somehow it just didn't seem like a wise move. I had never trusted the government normally and I couldn't see them taking any risk of the infection spreading further, let alone at the expense of their time and resources.

We saw the military set fire to cars with bodies in them, we even saw men playing, well taunting zombies, it all went very wrong very quickly, when one of the soldiers got bitten on his forearm. The other soldiers turned on him instantly, shooting him point blank in the head.

I've been lucky enough not to have killed one yet, well lucky enough not to have needed to. Though I did see Mike kill one in front of me when we were looting from the shop. The day after the military had swept through the town was the safest day to date with both me and mike getting a bit braver and taking a look round other peoples flats to see if we could find any water or food. We managed to get quite a few bottles of water, batteries and even some wine. It was going well until we walked into one flat. I instinctively shot to the ground as I heard the gunfire echoing throughout the room, we ran toward the stairs not stopping to look back. As I fell down the last few steps to the doors we tumbled out and headed straight back home. We ventured out again later, headed for the coffee shop which would usually be heaving, only because they gave away a cookie or cupcake when you bought one of their overpriced coffees. The place was empty, even the large coffee machines were gone, though I'm not sure how much use they would be without any water. At the start the looting was crazy. People were in the streets carrying TVs, stereos, even saw someone carrying a leather reclining armchair. There were no police to be seen. There were gangs of looters just grabbing people from out of their vehicles and taking their belongings. Mike and I watched this all going on from two small holes we left at the bottom of the boarded windows. As I sit looking at the last remaining food and water, I know what I have to do. I'm sure the dog is dying, she hasn't had anywhere near enough food or water over the last few weeks and has barely moved the last 2 days. I haven't even looked in on her today. I have a pit in my stomach not from hunger but from my impending doom, what will I find on my quest for food? Survivors are willing to do anything to survive, anything not to become one of those flesh eating creepers. Some of the things I have seen I feel disgusted, couldn't imagine how a human being could act in these ways. Though I never imagined we would be living like this. The small gap in the boarding in the window up until now was my only connection to the outside world. I want to go down and see what has happened to Mike and hate myself for being useless, that has been eating away at me for weeks now. I just want to be sure but can't quite bring myself to open that door, the noise must have been a creeper, and I assume it must have killed Mike then he must have ended up wandering aimlessly like the rest of them.

The only weapon I have is the baseball bat Mike kept by the main door to the apartment. I haven't got that much strength now but I know if I had to defend myself I would find the strength.

In some strange way I feel better just from writing this.

First thing tomorrow at sunrise I will go on the hunt for food.

Janine Markham 23

New York City

Notes found in Washington USA

When it happened we were in the middle of packing for Europe for a long break, we'd saved for months. We were both so excited Bobby answered the door to who he thought was the taxi cab driver but there was a man holding a boy up-side down, his hand and legs were tied. The man had a gun and told us to help him. at first we didn't recognize him but he was our neighbour. The blood covered his face and body. he knew Bobby was a doctor and had treated his son before. Jimmy explained he didn't know what it was and both of us didn't have a clue what was going on. The man explained that his wife fell with a virus and then went crazy and had bitten their son. He tearfully explained to us how he had to kill his wife. he said she was rabid and how it was not her anymore. And how the boy started to show signs of a sudden flu and then he died.

There were no physical signs of a pulse, but he came back to life within seconds, his eyes were white, enlarged and blood shot, it was not him anymore. he was lucky enough to restrain him, with nowhere else to go he came straight here. We turned on the news; there were reports of some crazy shit all over the world. The man then forced Bobby at gunpoint to examine the boy. as he put his hands under the boy's neck to support it, he lunged forward and bit Bobby, and within a few minutes Bobby had turned. The man aimed the gun and fired two shots Bobby fell to the floor instantly and the whole thing seemed to happen in slow motion. I remained calm and said to the man don't worry you had to do that, as he put the gun down on the ground. I grabbed the gun and shot the man then the boy. they didn't even have time to know what was happening. I dragged their bodies outside the house and then ran to him. Bobby was still moving. he took a shot to the chest and to the side of the head (his ear was hanging off). He was up and trying to get at me instantly, the shot to the chest must have stunned him with all the commotion, I didn't even realize he was completely blown apart. I shot him in the kneecap and he went down again and started to crawl toward me. Monster or not I wasn't going to kill Bobby, if this was happening all over then surely there must be a cure.

I took lead from the misfortunate neighbor and started to tie him up making sure I didn't get bitten. I even put a bucket over his head to stop him biting me. he kept wriggling and growling all the time, the noises sent shivers down my spine. I looked again on the news, there were more reports of strange occurrences, reports of a virus like rabies which started with flu, there were reports of water being poisoned, reports of terrorist attacks, each news broadcast contradicted the other and no one knew what was really going on.

It was surprisingly quiet outside, there were only a few houses in the vicinity, but I could see people from the door outside Bobbies place. I could only make out one person there that I recognized Mr. Balfour. I saw one of them smash the door in and go inside. I decided to start securing the house. I moved furniture in front of doors and windows. I heard a knock and some screaming at the door but couldn't make out who it was. I kept listening to the news until there were no broadcasts to be seen or heard. The noise from Bobby didn't bother me anymore. I managed to make it quiet by covering his mouth as much as I could and stayed upstairs. he was tied to the refrigerator with rope from his feet and head from the side it still looked like my Bobby, not from his right side his ear was hanging by a thread but I could not touch it. When I made a drink or food on the coal fire I always made two of everything. I did not waste the food I ate it myself. We had enough food and water and our basement was full of the stuff. Bobby was always saying how much shit was in the water and how it had to sit in an unclean water tank in the loft, which probably had dead birds in it, so we always drank bottled water. If I see another mini pack of raisins or eat another

I will cry. we had so many of them Bobby did work for the company so got free mini packs neither of us would really eat them like that but I would make cakes or puddings with them in.

Days went by the food and drink slowly started to go down. I talked to Bobby all the time kind of how you would with a sick patient. There were moments he looked at me and I swear I got through. I started to re-tell stories of our holidays and how we met. it has now been 30 days there is no change in Bobby he has stayed the same with no food or water. he never sleeps when I'm awake I don't know if he sleeps when I'm asleep. Today I got brave and took his mouth cover away and gave him a moldy steak that was at the bottom of the defrosted freezer. He seemed to do something with it but it looked like he had trouble swallowing it. I poured some water in his mouth and over him then covered him up again.

We were low on food. I went for a walk outside until I saw two of them walking toward me. I ran into Mr. Peters house there was no food at all anywhere so I checked over the road, still nothing I got to the surgery and climbed through a broken window. there was nothing there, no meat, no food from the main kitchen and I jumped up in the air an arm reached out toward me. it was one of them it was missing its left arm. I managed to get out alive but I had a scratch on my hand. afterwards I thought nothing of it. I started to run back up my path. I went to the kitchen and using a bread knife to cut into the arm just below my shirt. it was hard to cut and wouldn't go through the bone easily. I was sweating and felt feint and shaky. I poured my ration of alcohol over the wound and in my mouth I managed to find an axe from Bobbys tool box. it was not easy but I got through the bone and even cut higher so it was cleaner cut. it would not stop bleeding at all I burnt the end and using a saw from the red hot coal fire. then covered it in more vodka. I slept for ages after that but woke up feeling better than anticipated. There was no change in bobby I hugged him carefully and talked to him and at that moment I realized what world it would be without Bobby he was not him anything but I was kidding myself I had given up I know the words that I wrote are for me it helps Bobby will be untied soon and I could not wish for anyone in the world to do it but him.

Tony Newton

Note found in Kansas City, USA
October the 13th.

the pain of the initial bite is bearable i hid it from the rest of my group by covering it with a glove. i dont want to die and I know what Id do if it was one of them i try to believe that it would all be fine but deep inside of me i know that wont be the case. it itches now hell it hurts! theres a kind of numb tingling throughout the whole of my arm right up to my shoulder this is getting worse by the second my vision is fading im hot clammy dizzy and I feel faint. my legs are beginning to feel heavy and weak. it like every virus in the world is reaching its peak inside of my body.

im dying this is now the end fuck you world!

Im no longer in control.

Somebody help me!

God Help me!

Diary account found October the 14th Boston, USA.

This town is unrecognizable, the streets remain but the life is gone! Blood, flies, rotting flesh and body parts that lay strewn throughout the streets.

Skulls are the remains of a life once lived; they are somebody's loved one, wives, husbands, children and friends.

The dead are walking corpses and are long gone from here. There's no one to infect, nothing good to feast on.

From the corner of my eye I saw a dog, he was frightened, and he cowered as he moved next to a sign saying "restricted zone".

My journey was pointless; I travelled for two days solid to get here, killing twelve of the infected on my way.

I have no family or friends here now, just memories.

Everyone and everything is gone!

Nowhere is safe!

I am a zombie although I'm not yet infected!

I'm Fucked!

I'm already dead!

Notes found in San Diego, USA.

October 2019.

It was early in the morning I was up ready for work when the news broke here in America. I don't know what time it was for others but I wasn't fully awake. It felt like a bad dream. I had to pinch myself. I had to check with the neighbors they could actually see this on the news too.

But it was definitely real!

I don't really know how I felt at first; it was a mixture of sadness, sorrow and despair, mixed with a feeling of anger. But also I had this strange feeling that I was alive. I was truly alive for once in my life! I had gratitude for every moment that I was alive. I enjoyed the little things; my coffee tasted like the best coffee in the world. The views over the park at the back of the house looked like a scene from a fantasy film. I had just started work, only three months before the news broke. I had trained for years as a lawyer. That was my dream job; a job that was well paid. With the money and an investment in hard work and time, I planned to go and live my dream life in Canada. Retire really early and live a kind of hippy lifestyle.

I feel cheated in some way. Most of my friends weren't in work. They had left university but said they were waiting for the right job, as if any work was beneath them. I didn't want to have a break in my CV. I would have taken just about anything but I got lucky, working for a good firm. I guess I'll never know what it's like to live in Canada. I have wasted so many years trading and studying since I left school. I could have been out partying like my so called friends; in a relationship, enjoying life, but no, I was a loner, a geek, a book nerd, who would sleep, eat and study.

Money has always been tight growing up, well after I was ten anyway. Before that we were kind of rich. It just seemed that way. Dad was a builder, he worked himself so hard. He idolised me and Mum.

We used to live in a big house, with a swimming pool, until Dad died. Then there was no money coming in, so we had to downsize. We lost the mortgage on the house. It was strange going from one thing to the other.

Mum was a different person when Dad was alive, she was happy and she smiled constantly with wide eyes. She would always smile through her eyes, but after Dad went, she was an empty shell of a person. She died when I was eighteen. I think she was holding on for me.

When Mum and Dad went it was really just me. I had family that I would see: aunts, uncles and cousins. I would always go over for birthdays and Christmases.

My dad's brother looked the image of my dad, so in a way it

felt like he was still there.

Before the news broadcast I always knew something would happen, I had a sixth sense really. There were rumours and theories of the end of the world. I thought it would happen in 2012, but I was wrong, along with the many. If I had to choose how the world was going to end, I think a zombie apocalypse would have been the last choice. Maybe hostile aliens were taking over the planet, a catastrophic climate change, a huge earthquake or tsunami, global warming or an asteroid wiping us out in one hit, killer robots, overpopulation or engineered drugs, any of these would have been a better way to go.

This could have been caused by any of those things, but no one can be sure. The accounts are vague but they say that it's a killer flu virus, spreading at a rate at which we've never seen before.

Once you're infected that's it. I really want to survive it though it doesn't sound that great living in the aftermath of this but I want to live.

The thought of World War 3 had always scared me…is this it? Will this be known as World War 3? The zombies (the infected) versus the rest of humanity. It's a war that I don't want to take part in. I've never really understood war, it is pointless. I wouldn't die for any country, cause or argument. Each and every life is so precious. War is stupid. Don't get me wrong, the soldiers are so very brave and it must be good to believe in your country that much, that you'd be willing to give your life for it. If we were being attacked, I would defend my country but when we are sending people to other countries to fight and lose their lives in a war that we have no business in, it drives me crazy. I think we should just send money instead of our troops out there. My cousin was sent back from Iraq in a box. I just thought, what a total waste of life. It ultimately wasn't his war to fight. But no one forced him into the army, not like in previous World Wars. He wasn't drafted in. It was a choice, what a crazy choice. He was one of those children who got into army cadets at a young age, guns the whole bit. I just hope for a while he was happy. I suppose the army takes you, breaks you down, then rebuilds you stronger, like a drone, a robot, ready to fight to the very best of your abilities.

I hate seeing murderers, killers, evil bastards alive, when there are good people dead. It's crazy. I never really thought about religion much, I did when Dad passed, then a few years later when Mum went. I thought of religion, it had always bugged me. I prayed when Dad went that Mum would be ok, that we could have a so called normal life, as normal as it could be. It never happened. Mum was on so many anti depression drugs, she was like a zombie herself most of the time.

I don't believe now, I don't believe in a god that is causing this, innocent children and babies will be affected, no, this is wrong!

If you could chose to know the day you were going to die, would you want to know?

No, you would be living around that day, making choices around it. You would be invincible up until that day came. This is what this feels like as the world crumbles around me, around everyone. It's just a matter of time before I/we die. The big question is, what will it be? A zombie biting me, and turning me into one of the raging dead, taking control of my body for it to be dragged around until it rots or gets battered to a pulp. Will I be attacked by these arsehole survivors, that look like they are from the film Mad Max? Will I die of thirst, hunger, get shot, stabbed or will I get to the point where I can't take these feelings anymore: the shaking, the nerves, the worry takes over, will I choose to end it? The thing is, I don't want too. I want to survive, and I want to see this world, albeit a new one.

I just wish I was stronger and had more weapons to defend myself. I know everyone is in this position. There will be people who are stronger and people weaker than me. I always thought that I would get married in my late thirties, have kids, the ideal family, a boy and a girl. My husband would be outside, playing ball with our son and I would be indoors having pretend tea parties with my daughter, eating red velvet chocolate cake. Then when the kids were in bed, me and my husband would cosy up on a rug in front of the large open fire, listening to jazz music. Well this dream is out the window now. I never really loved or could reciprocate love.

I suppose the only person I grew to love was myself. Ever since I was an adult I have had no one to love. I am confident within my own skin, but I just want to keep that skin.

What would the future have been like? This runs through my head daily now. Would it have got to the point where we never left the house, did every bit of shopping online, even your cigarettes and alcohol? Maybe used a virtual taxi for a virtual ride to your virtual friend's house? Having virtual sex with holograms doesn't sound that great. The whole social media side would have erupted. It's bad enough now, taking pictures of your dinner, but what would have been next? Here is Grandpa in the coffin with twenty likes on it. Virtual funeral services, you can work online whilst attending a funeral through a video service. Where the seats used to be in churches would be screens with our faces on them. I think money, well cash, bank notes would have disappeared. Everyone would have their own card linked to them, with their thumb print on and the thumb print would stop forgeries. It would have stopped people selling drugs, they could only trade them. Would cancer have been cured in my lifetime?

Diseases would have been cured before they even were detected. I imagine taking a pill, like a vitamin. We would take one pill a day that could stop anything, a cure all. Holidays on the moon would be a must. People living on Mars might move to Jupiter. You could eat a milky way on the Milky Way itself. The goods you ordered online are delivered through a Shute in the home that everyone has. Just lift the plastic container to reveal your peanut butter and jelly sandwich, followed by your favourite ice cream. High street stores would not exist. Malls would be high rise flats to deal with the overpopulation. Sex would not rationed, neither would you pay for it. With the new thumb card, computers would be with you where ever you went. Your mind would be connected to everything; our hands would be just for eating. If you didn't want the robot to do it for you, maybe you would get dressed up for a night in. Plastering make up on, getting ready to just sit wired to the internet. Apps would be equivalent to people, home cinemas would be the length of your living room. 3D is long gone, 4D, 5D TVs, haptic touch panels. Why not cook along with your favourite chef in your virtual kitchen, cooking at your virtual oven while you're trying to block out that talent show that never stops. People who can't sing still keep singing, there have been so many good advances in technology but they are not miracle workers. Who knows, it's fun thinking about it all. Maybe we were already at the end and we just didn't know it? Maybe we went as far as we could go after all; are we like the dinosaurs?

I feel jealous now of previous generations of people who were old and died naturally, who never got to live this horror. The worry is kind of going gradually day by day. People talk openly about dying but we are all dying inside thinking about it.

I have packed a bug-out bag, I always was a worrier. I always worried about stores running out of things, plus, one of my hobbies was camping. The kit has first aid items, the usual plasters, pins, band-aids, antiseptic wipes, flint and steel, matches, lighters even some dry food and tins, if we don't need to eat them here first. I suppose it's a choice only I can make, stay here or go and try to survive out there.

The wasteland out there looks unforgiving, smoke appeared the day the news broke. Helicopters, planes, you would see just falling from the air. Cars on fire zig zagged all over the roads and pavements. Blood was everywhere; it was not just blood, but body parts, entrails and guts, still warm.

I am the only one left, well me and my cat here. Everyone else went but I chose to stay, I really thought help would be coming. I am up high enough and the doors are boarded up, so none of them can get in. Some doors have been kicked in by people trying to loot, but my door is solid. They would need to burn me out and how they could get fire inside my windows at this height I don't know.

The main doors of the flat are awesome. I chose this building for security reasons in the first place. It has a metal lift, the kind you see in old loft apartments. I have put metal poles and even next doors furniture inside it, so it can't go up or down to get to this floor. There were eighteen apartments here, nine with residents in. The rent was high but worth it for the views of the park. Everyone went, I chose not to go with them. I even saw my neighbour get devoured within one minute of leaving the house. The look on his face was horrifying as one of them continued to munch on his flesh. He was in shock the whole time. And another got hit in the head with a baseball bat by a youth, just for fun. He wasn't even carrying anything valuable, the person just killed him because he could.

I really miss coffee and breakfast, that was my favourite meal of the day. I always had turkey bacon with two eggs, on pancakes with lashings of lush maple syrup on top.

I can just imagine eating that now, and a takeaway pizza. I would swap my right arm for that at the moment. I'm going to stop writing, there's not much ink left in the pen. It has been a while since I have written anything. The cat died, if he wasn't so bloody skinny I would have even thought about eating him. I'm so hungry I feel so weak, I hope help comes soon. I have made banners out of old bed sheets and put them up in here and next door. How long can the body survive without food? And just dregs of this foul brown water????????????

Karen Soanes

Pocket book notes found from October 2019. Unknown Location.

America.

Ever since I was a child the name itself would send a rush of excitement through me. I loved TV shows like The A team, The Cosby show, The Fresh Prince of Bel Air, authors like Stephen king and Ray Bradbury. I would make peanut butter and jelly sandwiches just to feel I was like a part of America and their culture. when my mum told me we were going to America the land of the free, the home of the brave, the big apple, home of the president, the apple pie, big burgers, guns, money, fame Hollywood, actors, actresses, big portions and TV dinners, I could not wait I almost burst with excitement it was a quick decision mum had always wanted to go to New York, so this year for Christmas shopping we were on our way, it was fun tweeting to my friends, posting on all the social networks that I was going to New York.

I would normally have a seaside holiday in a two birth caravan, for three nights once a year, ever since I was four.

This was amazing, and definitely the most exciting thing in my life ever, hands down

we planned the whole thing out in less than two weeks, we were going to stay in a four star hotel, which to me looked utter luxury and it included breakfast and an evening meal, a tour around Hollywood and a lot of shopping.

We packed our suitcases carefully, we took only the clothes that we were wearing, but took a few suitcases. I made a list of all the sweets, chocolates, corn bread and cereals, all the stuff that I wanted to bring home, I had a list from all my friends, they wanted to try this and that and after a few hours on the flight I was buzzing, every time I closed my eyes I could see me shopping buying cool clothes, eating ice cream sundaes that were like skyscrapers but then something happened a few seats back. Havoc happened there was a young lad about ten years old, he started shaking he was hot, he had felt unwell earlier on, his dad was ill and had to stay at home but he thought it just was allergies, apparently it wasn't! He blacked out, there were people covering him with cold face cloths and fanning him down, he was given pain killers.

A doctor checked his pulse then whispered into the mothers ear "he's gone", the mum screamed out the loudest scream I have ever heard then shook the boy continually until eventually the crew and some others managed to sit her down and gave her some brandy. Then it happened! The dead boy jolted up and bit his mother, he bit her face, then her neck and was taking chunks from her, the mother fainted, then a man grabbed the boy, the boy bit him the mum started to react in the same way as her son first showing the same symptoms then she changed completely.

The man who had helped started to turn the same way, they bit and attacked others spreading it, it all happened so quick, it was like some really bad taste in flight entertainment, before too long there was blood everywhere. A group of us managed to get up the front of the plane and started piling in the tiolets and locking the doors behind us!, People are franticly screaming and banging to get in. I'm here with mum and a young girl who was screaming "my mum!", "my mum!", it was a tight squeeze we've been in here for around thirty minutes, the timeframe is giving us hope as the pilot may be ok, I can feel it my stomach churning as the plane is moving in a strange way. Mum has not stopped crying she is just looking at me holding the girl telling her she will be fine. Mum grabbed me so tightly I couldn't breath and just said thank you to me, I asked "for what?" she said everything, the noises have stopped but I can feel the movement so all we can do is now wait and hope the plane lands safely. please god save us! I don't normally pray but please! Save us! I want to live so much!!!!!!!!!!!!!!

A notebook found in central London written on 1st of December 2019.

The Dead

The dead roam the land, no weapon in hand
The hunger and moaning eternal
Alone and in packs they hunt and attack
No one is safe from the end that arises
The smell, the blood, the fear all fade in one's own tears
Mistakes erased from the years gone by
Trying to stand tall, no law exists at all just wastelands
warzones that are growing by the day
The rotting flesh walk and prey on the innocent
in time they will demise, no doubt many more will rise
Faith, hope and love keep us going
but without food or water we are nothing
The lives we once lived are no more
But who and what are we really fighting for?

Rotting Corpses

We are starving
They are starved
We both crave food
Though the infected crave only flesh
Death has become a way of life
The living dead rise

Walking around derelict, blood-stained streets
Blood hazed eyes
Rotting corpses on floors

Wasted hours are no more
No more hipsters,
senseless fashions and make-up trends
Cigarettes chugged down the latest mocha coffee mix
No more fake lenses and selfies
No more bullying
No more envy
No more safety
No more sloth
No more lust
No more greed
No more gluttony
We are all equal now
No more racism, gangs and violence
No more politics
No more liars
No more pride
No more rules
No more law in place
No more warm cosy beds or comforting hugs and kisses
No more sex
No more ghosts
No more false hope or consumerism
No more taking orders from people in suits
No more factories
No more slave labour
No more holidays
No more take-aways
No more alcohol
No more religion
No more Gods
No more naivety
No more youth
No more life

No more fake heroes'
Just bodies with no souls.
The smell of death lingers in the air
We are the walking dead
No more memories
We now choose to forget
Just blood, wrath, anger, pain and hunger
We embrace death
Only then will we be safe
But only if we die a good death
No more dignity
No more
No more
No more!

Soulless Soldiers

Evil, stricken before our eyes, sunken soulless beings that have no remorse

Covered in rags, worn down to their bones, cries for help drowned out by their groans

Crying has no place here, along with the weak, a safe place is all that we seek

The smell is so awful, the rotting remains, the dead are walking and eating our brains

Waiting for them to rise up again.

Infection

One breath
Either shallow or deep
One drop of saliva

One drop of blood
Just one bite
The infected are here
They outnumber us
We are the minority

Into the wind our ashes will fly
Erased are our bodies
No one left to cry
I am dead though I walk and I breathe
I have blood in my veins though I feel no pain

The world has been taken from us
In the blink of an eye
No one here is living
We've watched our loved ones die
Imprisoned in this hell on earth
Our fate is set in stone
We cannot win this war
We will all die alone.

Gone

Murder, death, blood and guts
No sunshine or forget me not's
Things that were once free have a high price to pay
Like walking in the park or the dawn of a new day
They approach us, death in their eyes, no see you later or
    goodbyes
This is final, the end, we've lost our loved ones and our best
    friends
This is the one thing left on which we can all depend
Blood fills the street with every heartbeat

Racing, running, no place to turn, money gone, no place left
    to earn
Life as we once knew it has been stolen from our souls
Women, men and children running to no end
Scared to death, their fate now is sealed
No one will be spared, they will all be killed again and again
A weapon is our only friend, I never foresaw this as the end.

One More Kiss

Eyes of blue, hair of golden sun, lost to new eyes, it cannot be
    undone
Skin once soft and golden now decaying and rotten
Heart which once felt, loved, now rotten with flesh so blue
Lips which once kissed now scarred, battered and bruised
One more kiss, my heart skips a beat, this kiss will be the last
Zombies surround us, no one can escape from this awful fate
Weapons of mass destruction may be our only option
No one knows how this will end
Children cry as men pass me by with missing limbs
No one daring to look each other in the eye
He who has the best weapon wins
Though you need to keep your brains to make it to the end.

Survival

The skies are not as black as the hearts we now posses
It's every man, woman and child for themselves
We hunt, we steal, we wound and we kill just to survive
No law, no control, we have lost it all
Even faith has no place here now
Our dreams shattered and lost in time

Memories cloudy, it's getting harder to remember
The love we once knew
No one here knows where the hell we're going to

This is not my body or the one I once knew
No warm fuzzy feelings, knives go straight through
Looking through new eyes borrowed from the dead
I killed this person, I am a parasite
I bring life where God should have taken charge
The infected, the humans, you go hide
Flesh is what we are after no substitute will do
Infection rages, sickened others weep, watch loved ones suffer
Flesh rots earth covered walking corpses
Much blood to be found but no flowers
For the dead just a bullet in the head.

The Walking Flesh

The flesh creep
The flesh walk
The flesh shuffle
The flesh eat
They never talk
The flesh always move
The flesh kill
The flesh will be our demise
The flesh, death in disguise
The flesh wants to devour all
The flesh needs us
The flesh wants our brains
The last of our remains
Please spare me
I want to live!

Death

Death screams, love kills, love heals, death lives
from beyond the grave are we the master or now the slave?
Rage to rabid, moans and groans, guts for glory
Bones now remain rotting decaying flesh
screaming silently from within, is to kill a sin?
Some lurk from below, some lurk under the skin
How did this virus start?
How will it all end?
How can a heart so broken ever begin to mend?
Just don't get bitten, don't get infected,
keep your mouth covered, don't let the blood contaminate
    yours
Don't let them bite you, don't let them bite,
don't let them bite, don't let them bite you
Don't let them bite you
Run
Hide
Keep running
Be invisible
Pray to god!
It's all we have left.

Infection

Beginning to turn
Pulse racing
Heart pounding
Silent screams
From within
Numbness
Shortness of breath

Eyes blurry
Going deaf
Hot, hotter
Sweating out sins
Head aches
Burning blood
From within
Trying to fight
Trying to stay alive
Clinging on
The last fragment of life
Virus here soon
My body the host
To the infection
I'll be a walking corpse
Soulless
Disturbed
Virus carrying demon
Soon!

By Carly Smith 17

Email from October 10 2019.

Hi Tom,

This message is being sent with much love and in the hope that you will receive it. There are rumours that the internet will be down soon, I don't know how much of this is true but be aware that it could go at any minute so get as much information as possible and contact friends and family while you still can. I didn't get a response from my last email to you but I'm really hoping that you are safe and that you and your family are as well as can be expected in this nightmare of a situation.

I'm at home still, we're kind of cut off here as you know but it's kind of a good thing. I went into the town today. We took the Molotov cocktails we'd made and threw them at them. They were on fire but still kept going, fire on its own doesn't kill them though it did slow them down a bit. When we'd thrown the Molotov cocktails at them we attacked a small group. We beat them to a pulp with baseball bats and knives. We have learnt that you have to destroy the brain, it's the only way of killing them! We've been trying to stockpile food and drink and I've opened up my house to a few families that I know from town and we're working together here.

If you can make it here buddy we can make room for you and your family. You are right in the heart of the city and they are advising people to get out of cities and large towns.

We have boarded the doors and windows and are trying to make a second barricade around the home. We are even converting the loft so that we can sleep as many of us as possible up there.

Medical supplies seem to be the hardest thing to come by. We are all going frantic as most of us take one form of medication or another. Jan is asthmatic and I have type 2 diabetes, this is really worrying. We are going out in teams later to check abandoned houses for medical supplies. Even the simple things like pain killers are hard to come by now!

Don't get bitten by one of them, it takes just a matter of minutes for you to die and then you will come back as one of those things. I've seen it happen right before my eyes. People here are fighting to survive. I saw a young lad attacking an elderly gentlemen for some tobacco. We went over to help but it was too late. He killed him for a small pouch of tobacco. This is crazy!!!!

I do have faith that things will get better, they have to, but I just don't know how long it's going to take.

Please take care mate and try to get here, safety in numbers and all that!!!!

Much love x

Trent Marsalis.

Email from 10th of October 2019.

Dear Sammy,

I've not heard from you today, all the rumors online are true as I'm sure you know by now this virus is spreading everywhere, as soon as I heard the news I went to your house but no one was in I assumed you were at work but there was no answer from the office!

I feel dreadful that the last time we spoke in person we argued, I'm so sorry I have text you like a thousand times since but I have had no reply. Sorry once again babe you know me by now, me and my jealousy, I just can't stand seeing you talking to other blokes, I just flipped when you sat on Clive's lap last night, I know we all had a bit too much to drink sorry once again babe,

I feel really sick to my stomach with worry that I will never see you again all I want to do is hold you in my arms. I'm sending this email from Dads place here in Camden, if you get it I'll be here till tonight. At least Dad's not leaving he said it would take more that the bloody undead to get him away from his apartment, he took pride in telling us how much money he had spent on his so-called bachelor pad, well he could fight them off with the pool I guess and the amount of Molotov cocktails he could make with his new bar! He'd spent around a grand just stocking it up let alone on the imported wood for it and marble that he had specially imported from France, I will have to go tonight I want to get to mum and Lucy to make sure they are okay it's a bit more desolate there so I hope they will be OK but I need to make sure, to be honest I haven't seen one yet but it's all over the news now and online, YouTube sites are saturated with sightings and police are out in force round here, they are shutting down stores and even closing roads. I will try to here as long as I possibly can. We even had the leaflet telling us to get out basically it doesn't look like we have an option, but we will hold up here until you come! Please get back to me and let me know you are safe, I love you Sammy stay safe sweetie love you babe!

Lots of love

Trevor Hogan x

Email from October 10th 2019.

Mark I hope you get this email I am at Stansted airport, we are locked in, its mayhem here. All flights have been cancelled. No one's allowed in or out, there are parents waiting for their children who are on flights. The planes are grounded with passengers in them. It has just been broadcast on the news that some kind of virus/outbreak has hit and we are in lock down here.

There are medical rooms at the moment where we're all being checked for symptoms. If you have a fever or are showing any flu like symptoms you are escorted to a separate area, though everyone here seems fine and we haven't heard from anyone in these quarantine areas. The news is telling you to stay inside, but then another news channel tells you to leave the city? I hope you are OK and decided not to go into work today. I assume the trains aren't running either. There's a large police presence here and a lot of angry people. All the food court shops are shut and we are now on a rationing system where pregnant women and the elderly are prioritized. We seem to be some of the lucky ones. Its chaos and the sleeping arrangements don't sound great either, the floor is cold and there are no blankets or anything. We have been told that we should wait here till further instruction. I don't mind as I don't know what I would be walking into out there.

I have sent an email to Mum and Dad but have not heard back from them, doesn't look like I'll be getting to Paris anytime soon! There have been major reports from Paris already saying that no one can come in or out of there, I bet all the important people aren't being treated like cattle, like we are. I bet they are on their private jets and into safe zones. Please try to let us know where you are as soon as possible, take care I love u xxx

All my Best Roger.

Journal Found Unknown location.

My sixteenth birthday I can remember it well. Mum and dad handed me this ticket, it was for me and one of my friends (and mum and dad of course) for a three night stay on a really posh sleeper train to Scotland and back including a stay in a hotel and sightseeing. I was thrilled the only other holidays we had before were a week at Clacton or Southend on Sea normally in a damp wet and smelly caravan, this was awesome. My other presents seemed insignificant to this mainly smelly bits and shirts, I wasn't into gaming like moist of my friends I was into reading mum knew one of my all-time favourite books was Murder on the Orient Express this was a real treat. The only problem I had was who to take with me, my friend Carl was nice he was a bit mad the kind of friend whose a compulsive liar normally bragging that he had sex with around ten people on his holidays or he got into a fight with a man twice his size it was all bullshit we knew this but we found it quite entertaining and used to laugh about it behind his back. Carl was my first choice but back up James was my all-time best friend he was kind of geeky mate with thick rimmed glasses and even a coat like Paddington bear, long curly hair that he would sometimes have in a ponytail, he was like a techs computer geek there was nothing he couldn't do on the computer he loved to hack we used to love hacking into security webcams and really annoy the operators, he even hacked into the school system and changed his test results he was that good. I had a lot of faith that if he applied his skills for good he could easily be the next Gates.

I asked James he said "yeah, course I would love to come it would be an honour". James was so polite and my mum and dad loved him, he wasn't the guy who took drugs or smoked stood outside supermarkets at night being a pest he was in the zone online most nights he would play online gaming.

The day came round really quick we got a cab to the station and then got the train. I felt like I was entering the orient express, getting on board I wore a sports jacket, even waist coat, shirt, smart trousers and my best shoes James wore his school trousers and a white shirt that was either his dads or another cast off from his brother. Mum and dad made the effort and looked really great though dad didn't look much different than he always looked he wore a suit for work.

We were greeted with huge smiles as we boarded the train James said to me "I feel like we're going to wizard school". I chuckled. We had two separate rooms me and James were in one and mum and dad in the other. We unpacked it was only for three nights but at the other end we were staying an extra night in a hotel, food was extra but we planned to go full board and have breakfasts, lunch and dinners and even drinks whenever we wanted, dad lit a cigar and said I might try a crafty one out of the window, the windows opened like they used to on old trains you pulled the window down. Mum stopped dad smoking and said there is a stop in half an hour you can have a smoke then. We walked down to the buffet cart and all sat there having coffees, cakes, sandwiches and biscuits, I had never seen so much cream or cucumber in my life.

We came to a stop, tons of people came aboard the train, dad managed to get his smoke and we were informed the next stop would not be for over an hour. After we ate we went back to the cabin, James lay on his bunk and played on one of his hand held games and I got deep into a book. Fifteen minutes later there was screaming coming from one of the cabins, dad rushed in to check we were ok then went to investigate. I joined him, everyone was screaming and coming our way there was blood everywhere. We saw a man bite a women on her neck, the man who bit her looked like a vampire attacking. The woman dropped to the floor the man was pushed into his bunk and the door closed tight behind him. A man checked her pulse, she was confirmed dead. One of the workers on the train covered her with a bright white sheet, blood soaked through where the wound was. as we were about to go to our cabin the body just rose up she stood up with her mouth open wide her eyes were so red with blood you could not see anything but blood she attacked the train attendant biting down on her arm the screams were terrifying The attendant went white then just fainted dad grabbed me and we pushed past the crowds that were forming behind us. We got through he grabbed mum and James followed us into dads cabin where we locked the door behind us but I couldn't stop shaking. James said "holy shit, there fucking zombies... real zombies"! Mum shouted "what the hell was that"? Dad replied "she was dead, the women was dead"! "She came back... her eyes had changed and she just bit into that women as if she was a snack"! Mum was panicking and started to pack her stuff up, "We need to get the hell out of here"! There was so much screaming from the corridor, James said "Why is the train still going"? "We need to get the fuck off. "Dad pulled out his smokes and sat back in the bunk smoking no one said a word, after smoking he opened the door and quickly shut it, it was mayhem everyone was covered in blood there were pieces of flesh all over the floor, dad opened the window the train was going so fast he said we could not jump we would be killed instantly, there was no chain or emergency chord to pull, all of us were panicking. We made each other worse dad was the calmest out of all of us mainly because he was chain smoking and handing out miniatures of whiskey. We all gulped one down I even asked for a smoke but dad said "Don't push it, it's a filthy and disgusting habit I wish I never started". Dad seemed to change becoming more assertive after that. He opened the door, there did not seem to be any humans (well normal ones) left, all The infected were feasting on The dead up to five on one body or more, most of the infected seemed to be distracted with feasting on the human flesh dad told us to creep into the next cabin and look out for anything that could be used for a weapon. There was nothing in the cabin, we carefully went into the next cabin there was blood everywhere but we hit the jackpot there were two large umbrellas with steel ends and a large wooden walking stick (ok not the best weapons in the world but at least it was something) James didn't have a weapon dad told him to stand behind him and look out behind him in case any come from behind. We moved on forward the next cabin had one of the feasting on a dead body flesh blood and guts were everywhere I felt instantly sick, we creped past the cabin and went unnoticed, the next thing I knew I felt a pull at my top from behind it was James he was silent but white as a sheet, as I looked round I could see a zombie biting his shoulder but James said nothing, he didn't even scream, dad pushed the zombie away from him and hit it, even placing the end of the umbrella into its heart, it kept moving, in the end dad was pounding the sharp point into its head. We were making a lot of noise and getting noticed, a load of them came at us, we all ran for the back of the train, mum screamed, one that was on the floor pulled her ankle and took a bite, dad screamed, attacking every one of them he was waving the point of the umbrella around, I hit one in the head, then we took turns stamping on its head and lunging with the wooden cane, finally its head was just mush, pieces of bone and flesh spread all over the floor.

dad was it the thick of it and when I turned around he had over ten of them around him i screamed at him to hurry and called mum then one came at me from out of nowhere it was James his eyes were blood red and he was rabid I hit him in the head it didn't do much I managed to push him into the cabin and lock the door dad shouted back mums gone she's gone now sorry son

I could not bring myself to look at her, I didn't want to remember mum with those eyes, with that look on her gentle loving face. dad shouted get to the back of the train and wait there, and I did. I ran shoving them out the way, they were slow and clumsy and weren't so scary on their own, than in hordes, as I reached the back of the train there was a large metal door that only these old trains had. There was a chain, I managed to break it off and open the heavy iron door, it went loud as the sound of the wind hit the inside of the train I nearly fell out with the force, I managed to get outside and pull the door behind me, I waited for around twenty minutes it seemed like five hours or more, I was numb no thoughts were going through my mind I was just existing, I had not seen dad for all that time so I opened the door it was a mistake there were tons of them as I was about to close the door I saw him dad looked bigger than he ever had before and scary he had never scared me before I only ever felt safe around him I didn't cry I just shook my head closed the door, the only thing on my mind was surviving, I was going to survive or at least I was not going out like this. I stayed there, we were going past stations that even had people on, I screamed at them for help but nothing, no one noticed me, nothing the usual business crowd, the type of people when you ask them the time directly to them, they pretend they did not hear you and walk on.

In the end the train stopped, my heart rate started to go down and I took a long deep breath in, I looked around the corner and saw the driver get off, he had been oblivious about the whole thing, everyone rushed up to me I was covered in blood, I didn't even notice, I was helped onto the platform, then it happened, all the passengers in there suits, holiday makers, children in their school uniforms started to get on the train, there were no buzzers for the doors, just those heavy metal doors you could open at any time, I screamed no!

No one listened. they got on the train, within a matter of minutes, It was total mayhem, the train stayed stationary, the doors stayed open, the infected came off and attacked people at the platform, the number of infected started to rise, as the ones who entered the train were turning before my eyes.

I ran up the stairs to the exit of the station as quick as I could, I was telling everyone "Don't go on through the station, don't. "Ninety percent of people ignored me, but some listed. I decided to say there was a bomb on the station, every one of them ran back. "Bomb!" I shouted, I continued to run and run, there was a police car, I got inside, and told the police man what had happed, he said wait there I'll check it out l said don't get out the car, as he was about to open the door then a body hit the windscreen. He reversed and we got the hell out of there, we got back to the station, it spread so quick, cars crashing and smoke in the background. on arrival at the police station the officer locked the station doors behind him, he did a complete check of everyone in the police station making sure none of them were hurt or infected there were a few who looked like they were at an afternoon football match, that had turned into a major turf war fight, cut faces, bruises and puffy eyes but none of them were infected.

The day I entered the police station was exactly twenty days ago, since boarding that train, I lost my mother my father my best friend and met proper heroes, people who have helped me through it. no one in our group have left the premises since, no one has been injured, we are all hungry and if I look at another vending machine snack bar again it will be too soon, I long for a hot meal and fresh air, and a hot shower, who would have thought I would be in a police cell shared with two others, for entertainment I doodle and write, this on a police man's notepad. it is total carnage it hit everywhere the world, no supplies are coming in or going out, I don't know the food situation exactly but we get our daily ration of chocolate, weak tea and cold beans or peas, it depends on the day, the first few days weren't bad it was hot meals from the canteen a lot has changed since then, we made some weird decisions we are a group, no one person is in charge there is no rank, it works, there has been some heated debates, but we all have something in common, we all want to survive, we all chose to not let anyone into the building, women, men, children the elderly, we have watched then on camera, all die because we would not let them in, we did not want to compromise and don't know how you get infected other than a bite, who knows what the future holds for us, I hope it is unity and this urge to survive this.

Welcome to world war 3.

–Dean McCarthy

Phone conversation 09/10/2019

06:03am

Sarah: I miss you, John, can't wait until you're home for Christmas! Me and the kids are so excited, they've started their advent calendars and Jodi's put a big, bold circle around the window of the 24th of December with a permanent marker. She's more interested in the countdown to Daddy coming home than the countdown to Christmas, it's not right without you here, John, I can't wait to see you again.

John: Thanks, baby that's just what I needed to hear. I miss you three so much and trust me you're not the only ones counting down the days!

We're supposed to be here fighting a war but at the moment we're mainly helping aid-workers and nursing staff around the camp. Viruses are common over here but there's a really bad one doing the rounds at the moment, the side effects are horrific. I've never seen anything like it before. It's scary. I'm really struggling seeing children as young as four dying from this, I can't help thinking that it could be our little Sammy or Jodi lying there. I'm helping out as much as I can but nothing seems capable of stopping it. We're adhering to all safety measures including using masks and sanitization to stop it spreading but quite honestly I can't wait to get out of here.

Sarah: Thanks for that, I really don't need something else to worry about! I've been worried enough about the Ebola outbreak and now this!

John: Don't worry, babe, I'm safe but it's still spreading rapidly here in Iraq. They're talking about shutting down transport links to attempt to contain it. I'll be back before you know it, really can't wait.

Sarah: Stay safe, I'll speak to you soon. Love you lots, honey.

10/10/2019

08:85am

John: It's a war zone here, they've now suspended transport links and four members of our unit have become infected. They're in the med unit under close guard and the rest of us are being given antibiotics to take as a precaution that should stop us catching it.

Sarah: It's just been on the news! It says that a flu-like virus has taken the lives of hundreds of people. You're worrying me sick!

John: Can I speak with the kids?

Sarah: I've just taken them to school. I'll put them on to you as soon as they're back home, speak soon.
    I love you...

John: Bye, love you too.

10/10/2019

13.30pm

John: I love you. Sarah, I really don't feel so good. I'm hot and clammy, my eyes are burning with a temperature. I'm worried that I'm coming down with the virus, the symptoms are the same. Sarah, I'm so scared, I wish I was with you right now.

Sarah: John, where are you?

John: I'm in the barracks, resting on my bed. The room's spinning. I've taken some aspirin and I'm drinking plenty of fluids. I just hope I'm fit enough to fight this.

Sarah: Get to medical bay now!

John: It's mayhem here. I'd probably die just waiting to see the nurse! Besides I can't move, I feel too ill. I have a cold sweat and can't stop my teeth from chattering. The light from the monitor is really hurting my eyes. I'll have to try and get some sleep. I feel so sick, my throat feels like its closing and I've got such a bad headache.

Sarah: I love you, John. Get seen by a doctor now!

John: Sarah, I love you so much. You have to tell the kids that they're my world. I love you more than anything sweetheart. I can't focus at the moment. I'll have to go now, I feel so weak.

Sarah: Stop talking like that! Go and get help now! I can't do anything from here, I feel so useless. Please, John, is there someone I can contact for you. You need medical attention.

John: You can't do anything from there, honey. I feel so bad, baby, I don't know if I'm going make it. Please listen, you need to know this, I have loved you from the very first moment I set eyes on you. You and the kids are everything to me. I have to go, babe. I can't talk anymore, I feel too ill. I feel too sick.
Oh God! I feel so bad... I love you...

Sarah: John, take deep breaths. Don't go to sleep, scream for help!

Sarah: John are you there?
John answer me!
John listen to me!
I love you so much! I need you, don't do this to me
John... John!... John!......... John!
No......

Papers Found in Wales.

Today I killed for the first time! It was a woman, she was wearing a large jacket that vaguely resembled a security outfit. she had a large diamond wedding ring on. as I lunged the hatchet through her skull and directly into her brain, I thought of the woman she once would have been, not as the rabid monster she now was, her eyes were blood red, and soul less, but running through my mind was a mother, a sister, a daughter. she like all of them did not deserve to die in this was. I know she was dead before but the shell still looked human. I am still haunted by the lady, all night as I lay there tossing and turning I could visualise her with her family as she used to be.

I could see the ladys husband running through the streets frantically trying to find her. the thought of him not knowing he was wasting his time maybe putting himself and others at risk to see his wife for just one last time to just hold his wife in his arms.

I would give anything to give my girlfriend jenny one last hug and kiss. watching Jenny die in my arms was the worst experience of my life I think I am selfish for thinking this way I was sick to my stomach when she went the future that we had mapped out was destroyed in an instant for the first time in my life I actually felt alone and scared.

We were together for over seven years we were about to get engaged I had planned a surprise at the end of the month in Paris.

Jenny didn't come back as one of them I wished she had in a way. I would have restrained her maybe put her in the garage or somewhere secure, scientists may have found a cure in the future, it matters not now.

On the day it happened we ran for the car, Jenny fell I thought nothing of it until I looked back at her on the floor. I ran to her and cradled her as I was stroking her head with my hand covered in blood one of them had already started to rip the flesh from her legs. I did nothing at first I was in shock, I just sat there with her in my arms, the curb was covered with blood her head cracked open on impact with it and the heel was broken away from her shoe. I felt a push on my back, I went to the side and there were gunshots fired. I was ushered away by two men in army uniforms they tried to get me to leave. I had no reason to live now, let alone leave with them. I walked past the dead, some walking, some not and past hundreds of screaming and panicking families. people were trying to get my attention, I just ignored them, everything seemed a blur as if it wasn't really happening. I walked back in the house as I looked out of the window, I could see Jenny, she had six of them feasting from her remains. one of them had her brain in his hand, well most of it, he took a bite like it was a melon. I watched until she was just a pile of debris on the floor, it was not her now, tears ran from my eyes as I watched in sheer horror. I could feel myself not blinking, just looking at the horror from the window. the army were outnumbered, there were too many of them. they tried smoke bombs, batons, guns and shields but the numbers of the undead just grew. there were even more screams, civilians were just blinded and walking straight into the oncoming clutches of them.

it's strange some of them seem to look more human than others. some have all their limbs and apart from their red eyes and predominant veins throughout their body, they could pass as a humans on their way to work in a busy street, you would not even look twice. most of them have their guts and organs hanging from their bodies, some have maggots crawling alive over them., if you stared at one long enough I swear you could see it rotting, you can even see ones that have their skeleton or skull showing through. there are ones that drag themselves on the floor, because their limbs have been attacked or chewed, making them that way in the first place. they are far too slow to really be a big threat like that.

They travel in packs like dogs, they follow noise and seem to have an almost sixth sense where food is. I have seen over fifty two people get killed twenty of those deaths were from looters and thirty two were from zombies.

Everyone seems to change when they die as long as the brain is intact. I feel like a voyeur I watch but never attempt to interfere or help. I have locked the house down no one could get in if they did I would kill them and enjoy every minute of it. the looters are evil raping scum, I would love to get my hands on them.

I exist now, I have no family in this country. I live just to see out of morbid curiosity now how this will pan out, how will it end? I really thought at first it would have been dealt with better and quicker. my faith is slowly fading that the world could be restored to some kind of normality.

I have not met or spoken to anyone in over 23 days. the moans seem to fade into the bird song or the river running behind me. the screams have gone now, I scavenge for food where I can, I have enough for a few days then I will have to go out again in search for more. we seem to have something in common we are both in search of food. I wonder when this madness will be over. Though it will never truly be over for me.

Notes found in Leith, Scotland

at twelve years old i never spected to see what my eyes have seen, there has been no real info for this happening it just sort of happened it has happened all across the globe from this morning all planes are grounded none in and none out no trains are moving in either direction i think we have got it here the worst at least i do not think it could be any worse im still numb my hand is shaking now while i write this i do not like writeing i hate reading but i want to survive i want others to help us we want to live.

the reports on the news of rabid people in sertan areas eating people taking a bite out of living human flesh, there were pictures online social network sites were going crazy with reports from all across the globe with videos that looked made up in emails it all looked fake mum told me to stay of the internet over the last couple of days but on my phone i was looking it all up there are so many theory as to what was going on the news did not say much. the internet did not say anything new today i doubt think they wanted to worry anyone, the local news was full of stories from fires road blocks stabbings to shootings and riots

im so scared im with my brother george he is shaking with fear he does not really know what to do, he was upstairs in his room when it happened to dad, we were getting ready to leave from the city we packed our bags we could only pack enuff stuff as if we were going by foot dad came back he was shot, we all tried to save him but we couldnt mum was still holding him, when it happened he turned he went crazy wed checked for a pulse and he lost to much blood to servive he was now one of them a biter a rotter a thing i don't think they deserve a name they are nothing they are soulless monsters.

i could not do it, my brother george had too, i had to pull

mum away from him, george hit him in the head with a vase it didnt work i grabbed the closest thing to had a metal pan and hit him it seemed to stun him but nothing my brother got his baseball bat from the bottom of the stairs

then ran up and hit dad from behind he fell down strait away he kept hitting him until he was no more, he was gone mum was in tears we did not know she had been bitten after a few minitis she turned with minites they were both gone, i don't know if there was more blood on the floor or tears from both of us, in a few minits it was over life as we knew it had gone we were on our own we paked up and began to walk away from our home we walked and walked and slept in the field under branches and trees a family let us into there house we told them what had happed we live here now we have been here for over a week no help had come but we are safer than we were we just wait now to see what happens.

i hope i do not have to wait too after killing seven people some living some dead, three men who tried to steal from me and ending my own brothers life once hed turned into one them, and three of the biters. i never spected to be liying here dying. it is that i am dying because i have no water. i had not been attacked by others or biten by one of them. i feel so ill, so weak and so tired. the heat is really bad though its ice cold and i haven't even had a sip of water for three days since my share ran out. im starting to see things things that are not really there and im dreaming of liying in a bath filled with cold clean water.

Notes Found in Philadelphia USA

I have survived here in the city for such a long time. There's no clean, safe water. I've had to travel to get clean water as no one will give you any. No one helps anyone now unless they get something in return. I offered to help protect people in exchange for water but they refused as I couldn't offer anything else. I put myself into dangerous situations, where other survivors tried to capture me unsuccessfully, they wanted my flesh and they weren't even the infected ones.

My head is making me feel sick with the intense pain, it's getting worse, it's the worst migraine, and I've had it for days it just won't go. I have walked for miles, I am away from any sort of civilisation which is a good thing, and I've only seen three of them in the last few hours. This house has been raided, even down to the wood being burnt, but there is some shelter here, just no food or drink. I don't know why but I hoped I would see a cow and that I would get a drink of milk from it. God, I don't want to go this way, I can't write much more, I feel too ill. I'm going to carry on, I have no option.

Tim Beacon

Journal found in Walthamstow London England. (Transcribed.)

Today I became a man. No one really knows what to call them…the infected…the undead…the risers…the walking dead or just plain zombies! Though they are nothing like the zombies you would see in a horror movie. They're much worse. They are so scary, and they look terrifying. They are so full of rage and the hunger, which they all possess. All they want to do is get to our flesh, though it doesn't seem to satisfy them, not like if you or I were starving and sat down to eat a three course steak dinner. We would be full and the thought of food would make us feel sick to the stomach. I have seen them devour one person then go on to the next and then the next, though most of the flesh falls down their chins and does not seem to digest properly. It must be like an ongoing hunger for them, never feeling full or satisfied. Each one walks a little different to the others, though they all shuffle; none of them could pass the drink driving test of walking in a straight line.

Today has been the longest day of my life. You know how Christmas day seems to just zoom by and the days at school seem to drag on forever? Today has just gone from bad to even worse.

Dad works as a doctor in the centre of London. As I was getting ready for school Dad ran in and told me to get changed, he said "you're not going to school today." It was then that I knew something was wrong. He'd never let me have a day off, even if I had flu he would make me go in. He would give me some story, saying about one of his patients, how they would be only too happy to feel the way I did. It worked, though it never used to make me feel any better. He was panting, this was out of character for Dad he was always calm in any situation. He started to fill a suitcase and told me to do the same, he even told me to get both of my asthma pumps and enough clothes for a few days.

I kept asking questions but he would just ignore them. As we ran
out of the house he handed me a plastic mask, at first I thought
he was joking but he was deadly serious. We both wore masks
and got into the car, we drove straight to the petrol station where
Dad filled the car up and a container too. We drove on to the
hospital, he told me to go with him, we kept our masks on the
whole time. It was mayhem at the hospital. Dad grabbed my
hand and pulled me in the direction he was going. He hadn't
held my hand since Mum had passed away but it was
comforting, even amongst the chaos that surrounded us. There
were hundreds of people crowded into the hospital waiting
room, lots of them screaming for help. The staff and security
could not control the situation. Dad walked into the hospital
canteen and called out to one of his colleagues, the man said "We
need more help, this is spreading at such an uncontrollable rate,
and it's definitely a flu type virus that has mutated." The man
then started to whisper into Dad's ear, though I could still hear
him. He said "You won't believe what's happening, they are
coming back to life after the fever takes control. When the body's
immune system can't take anymore, when the body can't fight
the flu, after they have died, they are returning but not as they
were. They have what appears to be rabies like symptoms. He
pulled Dad to the operating theatre, there were over thirty of
them all locked in, as we walked down the corridor we could
hear screaming, Dad shouted "we can't contain them here, not
with this amount of staff." Dad called his work colleague to the
pharmacy, he gave him 15 boxes of antibiotic and told him to
hand them out to the staff, he told him to take them immediately
and round up the staff. Dad handed me a bag full of antibiotics
and painkillers, dressings and butterfly stitches, he stood for a
while stroking his beard deep in thought, whilst he was doing
this the screams got louder. People were running down the hall.
Dad had a bin liner full of antibiotics and painkillers. He handed
them to a lady at reception, she was behind the glass. We joined

her in the small room.

Dad's colleague came back with other staff members but there were too many people to fit in one small room. Dad was informed by someone to cease distributing and for us to get out of there and for him to get back to work, but he refused saying that he wouldn't leave all these people to die. Some of them went back to work some stayed, Dad started to hand out the antibiotics and painkillers to as many people as he could. A man tried to stop him but Dad hit him. The man fell when Dad hit him, he got up and walked away and he never returned. When all of the painkillers and antibiotics had been handed out, we left the hospital, it was worse than before, it was the first time I had ever been this scared. Blood was dripping from the mouth of a zombie and I watched in horror as it bit someone. It started to try to eat a man's arm. Dad pulled me toward him, as we ran out of the building Dad was shouting for the staff to leave saying this is not our problem now, he was on his mobile ringing the police, he said he left a message on the answering machine, we ran to the car. A lady followed us, she worked at the hospital. She had a carrier bag and a handbag. She was covered in blood all over her uniform but it was not hers, she wasn't infected or bitten. She joined us in the car, it seemed to take forever to get on the road, it was mayhem, the roads were blocked with crashed cars, bodies strewn all over the roads, some people were trying to get our attention and get in the car. Dad just drove around and drove onto a field, we kept driving. As we started to get away it was eerily quiet, none of us spoke for the first few minutes. Dad drove carefully up and down bumps in the grass. The lady reached back and grabbed my hand, she said it's Carol and you must be Connor. I replied "Yes." But I did not want to chat I was scared to death. They started to talk but neither of them could fathom how or what was happening. We drove and drove for miles, until there was nothing but fields and trees, then it hit us there was a small river. It could only have been a few feet long but there was no other way around it. Dad stopped the car, we sat for a while, and then Dad said we should cover the car up and camouflage it and get back inside. It seemed like we were in there for days, time dragged on. It got late and we decided to sleep in the car, before that we ate crisps and some chocolate and drank coke. I slept through the night as I awoke from a bad dream with a jump I woke Carol up, Dad reached back and grabbed my hand to reassure me, we left pretty much after that, we decided to walk. It took a while to get over the small river but we did it. As we were crossing we could see one of them coming towards us, we sped up none of us had weapons on us. Dad made us all take the strong antibiotics. There were two types of antibiotics, they were huge and tasted bitter but washed down easy enough with coke. We needed weapons, we picked up sticks, they would have been less than useless as a weapon but at least they were something. We walked and walked, our feet were killing us. We came to another small river, there were two of the infected over the other side, and they spotted us. Dad walked around first, just as he got around they went to attack him, he jumped back to us, they took the bait and came for him, both were now in the river, we ran away from them and crossed further up the river, we kept walking. In the distance we could hear gunshots and as we got closer we could hear the loud roar of vehicles. We walked faster, as we got closer we encountered the undead, the infected, but were lucky enough not to get bitten. After walking and walking we encountered the army and police and we were stopped by them. We all had a sigh of relief when we saw them, they ushered us along with another group. We waited for ages inside a large army van, everyone was talking about what had happened and saying what they thought had caused this. After a while we started moving, we had two guards at the back of the van. They were shooting any undead they saw. We arrived at a gate and went in. We were treated like cattle and had to give blood and, if we could, a urine sample. We were given hot tea and clothes and all sat on the floor in the large tent. My phone was still on. As I write this my fingers are a bit numb, though I feel the safest I have in days. I think everything is going to be okay now, we are being guarded with guns, and Dad has just closed his eyes for the first time since leaving.

I'm being told I can't write or have my phone anymore for safety reasons.

So I can't write anymore!

Notes found Unknown location.

I never could have imagined this horror could exist in our lifetime. I have seen my fair share of horror in the army; I have seen my friends both young and old get blown into pieces. I have tried saving lives when they have been left with only half a body. I have had to scoop my colleague's remains from the floor. I have been chatting to people and seen them shot in the head.

The thing is, I signed up for this, to protect and serve!

The army were not ready, hell I don't even think I was ready, you're facing the unknown. This virus and the effects of it, rabid creatures that you end up being, are uncontrollable in their numbers. I don't know any more than anyone else really about the virus. They are trying to get a vaccine out, though, is it worth it now? There is no way of using it safely. The vaccine would probably get stolen by a gang of looters. And how many of the those that are fighting to survive would want to live with these memories replacing all they've cherished previously. The only way I know to eliminate them is by destroying the brain. I think most people know this by now, even on the first day you could hear echoes all around of people shouting out "destroy their brains, it's the only way to kill them."

What actually are they? Are they going to be the new us?

Are they the end?

Or were we the end all along?

I am a British military officer. I have seen a number of strange things, from parasites to neurotoxins. The parasite contained in the blowfish can cause the whole body to shut down and cause strange effects in the body. But I've never experienced anything even vaguely like this! I know there are people around the world doing stem cell research and making man made viruses as protection or for use in warfare. But the spread of this flu like virus is like nothing that I know of. The virus is clever, it seems to have no predictability to it. A lot of people are calling them zombies; we inspected a colony in Iraq where there were people who had very similar reactions to the flu. They were taken to hospital and put into safe units. I have had to eliminate many, be it young or old. After a while you switch off, it's not you doing the killing, ending lives anymore, you are a drone working on request of your superiors. It doesn't matter how much the army train you, how much money or pension or social housing you get, nothing can prepare you for that first kill, and the nightmares that haunt you for the rest of your days.

I have witnessed the use of hallucinogenic drugs in many forms and this, at first, felt like that, as if I had been drugged with acid and was hallucinating, and that this was not in any way real.

I'm afraid to say it is totally real.

We sometimes used code names to speak to one another, a code of our own devising. The unit was twelve man strong; I was in charge. One young recruit was chatting about playing games online, shooting games. Before he had his first kill he asked me if it would help to think of them as zombies. I told him to think of them as whatever he liked, just as long as it helped him to get through it. Every time an enemy appeared he would shout "Zombie!" then fire his rifle. It caught on. I think the whole of our team were basically playing a real life video game. It made it easier to delude ourselves and forget that these beings were real people with families at home; that they were fathers and sons, brothers and uncles. When we killed them we thought of it as a video game, im my head they were chractors from a game not human. It also took away some of the element of fear; it worked, we were the tightest unit that I have ever operated within. It was wrong, it stripped those who had been people, just like us, of any dignity. But it brought smiles to my unit and helped us function in a nightmare situation.

This year I lost my best friend – not from a bullet to the head, not from a bomb, not from being held hostage, not in any way resulting from carrying out our orders, but from the evil in our camp. John was gay; he was caught with another officer, who was transferred. It's funny how men, real, tough men can be such evil bastards. I heard them talking, it was as if they were still school boys. They were calling him abusive names, pushing and barging past and not listening to him, constantly belittling him, making his life hell. John hanged himself. I was the one to find him, and it affected me more than scooping up the remains of one of my team. I didn't expect to see it, I walked into his room, he shared a bunk. The other man was asleep underneath, completely unaware of what had happened. I pulled him down, I was sobbing. In this day and age, to end it all because you are gay is crazy. I have witnessed this kind of thing before in the early nineties, along with racism from both parties, but surely we have all grown, moved on since then. Perhaps I might have expect these views from the older generation, who literally don't know any better, but come the hell on!

I had just returned to my home country after a long period of duty, one of the longest of my career. My wife had changed her hair, it was much shorter. I loved it. I held onto her for ages, even after all this time I cannot stop the tears from streaming down my face every time we are apart. She does the same. I see her take a deep breath and a sigh of relief every time I get back safely. It must be living hell for her all the time. If I had met her before, if I had already had my son, I would have never joined the army. Enlistment should be a single man's game. My son had grown a few more inches, his face had filled out and he seemed bigger all round. I did not want to let him go from my arms, he had to prise me off him, just in case any of his friends saw; that really wouldn't be cool, for your friends to see you hugging your dad in public.

I was home for just a few days and I got a call, an answer phone message that I replied to. At first I thought it must be a prank but it wasn't. I was informed of the virus and its horrific effects. I didn't understand it, this wasn't normal; not the standard procedure. Every member of the official services was being conscripted. There were even TAs and volunteer police. I don't think we knew much before anyone else, it all happened so quickly.

I brought my wife and son along. I didn't want to leave them behind. Lots of people had done the same. The women stayed in a separate tent; a huge tented facility with tables, chairs, food and drink. My job was to unload the vans full of a potential flu cure. Approximately a hundred yards back was the other tent where they were introducing people who supposedly didn't have the virus. The ex-army barracks was put up in a day; surprisingly there was some order at first. People were in cuffs – both hands and arms. They were required to have their blood tested, as well as other routine investigations. Then things fell apart; they began to come out of the transportation rabid. Their heads would be moving frantically, jaws frenziedly snapping. Some of the vans we opened up contained two or three of them eating remains on the floor. We learnt then how to kill them. All of this was in a gated area. There were people trying to get in for safety. A few people ran over covered in cuts where they had injured themselves on the barbed wire. They walked straight into the clutches of the infected and ended up as food.

We were getting more help but still it wasn't enough, even though we were now only taking those who were supposedly fine. I changed clothes to man the defences. We had been told to shoot anyone trying to get over the wire, no matter what their condition. The undead couldn't get over the fence, they just leaned against it moaning and groaning and trying to get in. We shot whole battalions of them. But as fast as they went down, more replaced them. I had to tell desperate civilians to get down or they would be shot. They were just trying to get away from the infected. I hated following these orders – it was wrong. I shot over a hundred civilians. I stopped counting after that. It came to the point where we were just firing, one man per fence, shooting continually. I was called away and someone else took over my role as a killer. I lined up with around thirty other soldiers from different regiments. We were told to fire at anyone trying to get in the perimeter, then our orders changed, we were ordered to fire at the medical tents. The screams were the worst I had heard in my life. We must have fired over 10,000 bullets in all. The colour of the tent fabric turned from cream to claret within seconds. We could all see the holes in it getting bigger from the impact of the ammunition. I had been oblivious to what was happening behind us. There had been more breeches from the fence and the numbers of infected inside the safe zone were growing. I walked into one of the tents as soon as it was safe to. A young child ran toward me, a little girl, she had been hiding under a table which had come to rest on its side. She fell to the ground before she could reach me, I saw the bullet hit the top of her head, bullets were being fired at anyone suspected of being infected! I rubbed my eyes, this couldn't be real. My wife and son were on the ground, clutching one another, their mouths covered in blood. They had been caught in the crossfire, as I looked down at my wife I noticed the first aid tabard she was wearing, her and my son were trying to help in the first aid tent, I'd assumed that they were safe. They had bullet wounds to the head, I was in shock!

I hugged them both. I held them tight, one in each arm. I felt like I was watching through someone else's eyes. I heard myself scream. What was I doing? Had I killed them? Had I been the one that fired that particular bullet? Why did they have to be in that tent?

Another officer tried to console me. Before too long other men found themselves in the same position, their families gone. We were now protecting no one but ourselves. It was never exactly clear how the infection had spread. Someone who wasn't obviously infected must have got into the tent. I heard a rumour that an old man had a heart attack in there and then turned. We took everyone out of there – if you weren't wearing officers' uniform you were shot. Those in charge were not taking any chances.

Before long the fence gave in; it was inevitable. Three of us managed to get inside the old building. As we made our way in, Jim got hit on the back of the head by a survivor who had been hiding. The poor man was scared to death. Jim was bleeding from the head. I did what I had to do. As we penetrated further into the building the man who had helped kill Jim was attacked and bitten by a walking dead man. I ended it for him but the noise of the shot brought more of them. They took Nigel down and I had to shoot him too. I managed to escape by the skin of my teeth. Eventually, I came across a room, it was dark and cold inside but you could lock it. I reached for my water bottle and took a sip. There was a pack of cigarettes lying on top of a note pad and pen on a chair. I took one out and lit it. God knows I needed it! I quit smoking five years ago, but, boy was it good. I tried my phone. I wanted to get in contact with my parents and my wife's parents, but nothing, no signal.

I gathered everything I could to form a barricade and secured the door. From the window, I watched as more of the infected arrived minute by minute. The officers and army were rapidly becoming overrun and turning into more of them themselves. We were completely outnumbered.

I don't know why I am writing this really. I suppose I just want someone to know what happened; the last dreadful minutes. I want to say goodbye to my parents and my brother. They always expected me to come home in a body bag, but not from this, I'm sure. I could never live in this world. Things would never be the same without my family. The love I have for my wife and son is so strong. I shared my heart with them. I take comfort that they are now beyond any fear or pain.

Thank you Mum and Dad for everything. Thanks for being such great parents and for giving me your unconditional love. Thanks little bruv, I love you. I'm safe now. I will be with my wife and child forever!

It's not worth fighting. Just give up! Stop delaying the inevitable!

Commanding officer

Phillip Greene

Notes found in Suffolk England.

Day 1

It came over the internet at first, I thought it was a joke or the result of some kind of hacking prank, but it wasn't. I realized that when every single news channel was covering it. Nobody could tell us what had actually caused this, all we knew was that a global flu like pandemic had hit. As I watched the screen in horror it reminded me of the devastation caused by the terrorist bombings several years ago.

I watched the News as China, Russia, Australia, Sweden, France, America then the UK went red, that's when I panicked. That's when it hit me, we never really got the bad shit here like earthquakes and tornados, and I thought we were going to be safe but boy was I wrong.

We fled our home today, I can't stop myself from shaking and I'm drained both emotionally and physically. I need some sleep.

Day 2

I got some sleep, not much though as we (I and my partner Jaxx) took it in shifts through the night to stay awake. We slept in an old barn, it was deserted. We had no light apart from the matches from our smokes.

The internet is still up and running which I am surprised about, I have tried making contact with family members but have heard nothing. I'm getting worried and just hope that they are all safe. Jaxx managed to contact her mum and dad who said that they were being moved out by the army, so at least they should be safe for now.

We made the most of the little battery life left on the laptop today, searching for safe places to head. We saw them for the first time last night, it was just people running around covered in blood, and I was too scared to take a closer look. They don't seem to have the ability to move very fast but that doesn't make them any less scary. I think that the sheer volume of horror stories I've read and movies I've seen are not helping much right at the moment. There are bodies strewn about the place, people who have been killed in the crossfire between the army and the infected. We started to move on but i began to get dark so we decided to spend another night in the barn. We can't stay here again tomorrow as we don't have enough food and water supplies.

Day 3

Today we were awoken by a load banging on the barn door; it was still dark which made the situation even more frightening. There were around ten of them "The Infected" eerily groaning and throwing themselves against the barn door. We quickly got our shit together and grabbed some weapons to best defend ourselves. I had a pitch fork and Jaxx used a big heavy hammer. We bashed at the wood on the back of the barn, we'd managed to squeeze through the opening we'd made when one of them grabbed at Jaxx. I hit it three times with the pitch fork, but it was still going until I forked it in the head which did the job. Jaxx started to scream. I covered her mouth so that we didn't attract any more of them to our whereabouts, then we made a run for it. More of them were scattered around, as soon as they laid eyes on you they came straight for you. We had speed on our side, though we were so tired and even climbed a tree just to get some much needed rest.

We noticed a road; it was full of cars, coaches and buses, with a good share of blood and even bones, the remnants of friends, neighbours and fellow human beings. There were no signs of life. We walked along the road heading in the opposite direction from which we had come. We started to carefully check through the abandoned cars and busses for food and water supplies. I reached into one of the cars and a zombie lunged from the back seat, as it fell from the car we noticed its legs were missing. We both took turns destroying it, aiming for its head. Today we learnt how to destroy them, and it worked with the fork to the head.

It was then that we noticed something written in blood on the side of a van, it said:

YOU HAVE TO DESTROY THE BRAIN!

We managed to scavenge some half eaten chocolate bars and some water and cola to replenish our stocks. It seemed almost as if the darkness was instantaneous. We climbed inside a large truck and secured it from the inside and slept together behind the curtain, in the bed inside the truck. It felt luxurious in comparison with the barn which had been home for the past few days.

Jaxx thinks I'm crazy, but I need to keep a log of the horror we encounter, for my own sanity, it gives me something to do.

Day 4

We awoke around 6:00 am the next morning. Jaxx was smiling, she said "Look what I've got." It was a black bag filled with food. There was chocolate, crisps and even some boiled sweets but best of all was a can of beer which we decided to save for later. I moaned at Jaxx for going out looking for food alone.

Suddenly there was a loud bang, it sounded as if it was close by but it wasn't. We could just see the smoke, it must have been miles away. We walked and walked past the infected and past bodies. Jaxx made her first kill on her own. The roads weren't clear enough to drive on but we found an abandoned motorbike. We looked for the keys, finally finding them in a pile of blood and remains on the roadside. It felt kind of strange driving a motorbike with no crash helmet but even stranger driving through the remains of what were once people just like us. We drove to a small village with a small group of shops, chip shop, village butchers and a pharmacy; these had all been looted already and were now burnt out shells. We ventured into one of the surrounding homes, with no power it could have been war time. By now we only had one bar of battery left on the phone and the chances of hearing that family were safe and well were quickly diminishing. We retrieved nothing from the village but a baseball bat and a cricket bat, but it wasn't easy to carry them on a motorbike.

Day 5

Last night we slept above a florists. The shop had smashed windows but we were grateful that it wasn't burnt down inside. There was no food or drink but at least we could use the blankets and bedding. When we awoke today the phone battery was dead. I think I got more upset than I should have but it just felt like our only lifeline, our only connection to the world we once knew!

I don't know if the power is out everywhere but it certainly is here. We continued to move forward on the motorbike but it was getting harder and harder to manoeuvre around the bodies and the infected. We stopped for a while and shared our last cigarette until heading off again. After just a few miles a heard a gunshot roar through the air. I didn't stop in fact I sped up a little. Suddenly Jaxx let out an almighty scream. I couldn't turn my head without crashing into one of the strewn bodies so I shouted back to her "Are you alright?" "Yes." She quickly replied "Keep going." So I did, I wondered if she'd seen something, we were both full of unadulterated fear, I'd imagine the rest of the world were too, but something must have spooked her. Jaxx had her arms locked tight around me. We'd only been driving for around

15 minutes when Jaxx's head started to lean against mine. I slowed to a stop and realised that Jaxx's body was limp against mine. As I carefully got off of the bike Jaxx's body fell to the ground. It was then that I saw that she was covered in blood, she'd been hit from behind, and she was gone. I clung onto her tightly as I sobbed. I was truly alone now no one to look out for and no one to look out for me. I turned away I couldn't stand to look at her like this. As I debated what to do next I noticed movement out of the corner of my eye. I smiled as I reached out to her, that was until I noticed her bloodshot eyes. She lunged toward me, with her teeth clanging together. Jaxx was gone. She was one of them now; I hit her until she didn't move anymore crying a little more with each swipe. Wiping the tears from my eyes it was finally over.

After removing her ring and necklace I unsteadily got back onto the bike, still shaking and more than a bit traumatized, I just drove.

I'm safe now, I'm at an Army base. We're all alike here, we've seen things we could have never imagined and done things we didn't think we'd ever be capable of. We're all broken and we've all lost someone. I don't want to die but I'm not sure that I can handle the alternative. I want to remember Jaxx as she was and not that thing that she became. I was lucky to have spent the time that I did with her, perhaps I can be of help to others. I have offered to volunteer as a member of the Army, they've said they'll get back to me, there are no amateurs here, flu I don't think so!

Jaxx was fine right up until the last few minutes before she turned.

I think everything will be okay I got this far!

Blog post from October 2019.

I never imagined blogging about this…food, recipes, cupcakes and possibly e-coins but never the zombie pandemonium that we are currently facing. I don't suppose this post will be read by many people but I'm sad, angry and fascinated, just like everyone else. I'm lucky enough that I haven't been bitten or exposed to the virus and where we live, here in Scotland, we are well out of it. In fact it's a miracle we have the internet at all (though it did take a few years longer to get than everywhere else). We went out today, me and Father, to get any supplies we could. We had no luck. The shops in the nearby town were empty. I expected to see more of them, but we only saw one. It was a man; he must have been in his late 30s., His mouth was covered in blood and his clothes were ripped. He had a huge open wound on his arm. He was walking slowly and stumbling, and he came towards us and punched his fist against the car window leaving smears of blood behind. It was strange, seeing one of them for the first time. It was like encountering an alien. The main thing I noticed was his soulless eyes, vacant. He wasn't human, he wasn't like us, and though he wasn't dead, he literally was a walking corpse.

When I first heard the news from my dad I laughed. I couldn't help the nervous smile that spread across my face, and I couldn't stop the tears uncontrollably streaming down my face. Dad hugged me and wouldn't let go. First off Dad rang round the family, some of them he managed to contact but he didn't get an answer from most. The news was broadcasting the evacuation of highly populated areas. We tuned in to our local radio station where they were telling people to stay in and secure the property. In reality we couldn't have been in a safer area so we were quite lucky in that respect.

Each news channel gave a conflicting story; it seemed that the more information they were receiving, the less they actually understood this thing. Doctors, scientists and reporters were all saying that this had been caused by some flu-like pandemic which seemed to be causing rabid effects. There was no way a couple of aspirin was going to make this one go away!

Dad is starting to gather as much food and drink as he can (he's in the garden now, pulling up the vegetables) at least one thing's for sure – we won't be starving any time soon!

On our way back from the looted shop we stopped off at the police station. I'm not sure what we expected to see but it was boarded up from the outside and had been graffitied in red paint 'You bastards! Thanks!' We stopped at every house we came across after that. We tried to convince Mrs Jones to come with us but she wouldn't leave her pets and insisted that she'd had her life and her time was coming to an end anyway. She laughed and said that she had to go some time; it may as well be now. She gave us some bottled water and some fresh eggs from her chickens. As we left Dad reminded her that should she have a change of heart, she knew where we were. The next home that we approached was Mr and Mrs Vican's. Dad gave a loud knock on the door but nobody answered although the car was still in the drive. Dad kicked in the front door, they both lay dead on the floor, blood gleaming from the cracks in the white tiles. Dad told me not to look as he covered them with a sheet, but the shock didn't allow me to look away. They had both been shot in the head. I'm not too sure what happened, if it was suicide or if one of them had turned and been shot by the other who had then proceeded to kill themself. As Dad closed the door behind us I knelt to the floor and vomited.

I stayed in the car whilst Dad checked out the last house

before ours. I locked the windows, the silence was eerie and I didn't like being alone, but I just couldn't face whatever was lurking behind the door. Before long Dad appeared from the house with Mr Brafhail (he was an old man we chatted to daily). Dad used to do his shopping and give him fresh fruit and veg from our garden. Mr Brafhail came back to ours, he's asleep now, he seems to sleep most of the time. We took all the food and water he had, Dad even went back to get the shotgun with which Mr and Mrs Vican had killed themselves.

We've just fitted boarding up at all of the windows and doors, making the place secure. Dad even put barbed wire and broken glass around the window ledges. We moved all of the ladders and garden tools from the shed in with us. It's so dark in the house now, it's difficult to tell the difference between day and night. I spend all my time trying to get more information from the radio. There are no announcements yet, just websites teaching you how to kill them. 'Aim for the head, destroy the brain and don't get scratched or bitten'. There doesn't seem to be any fresh information. I can't watch the videos online, they're Fucked up and twisted!! Dad killed one today. It threw itself at the window continuously, so Dad shot it in the head before it could do any damage. He dragged the body away from the house. A few hours later 2 men pulled up in a car. They came crashing through the front door. One of the men was carrying a gun, he had an army uniform on which was covered in blood and the other had a T-shirt and his arms were covered in tattoos. They showed Dad a badge, stating that they were officers, but when they told us to hand over any weapons or food we had, it just felt wrong. The way they looked at one another put us all on edge, I could smell the alcohol on their breath. One of them asked to use the toilet; Dad showed him where it was upstairs and came back down. He struck whilst they were separated, putting his hands around the man's neck, he started to strangle him. I could see the blood rush to his head as he flailed his arms attempting to loosen Dad's grasp on him. He put up a hell of a fight but Dad didn't stop, not until his body was lifeless. Dad dragged the body into the kitchen and took the gun he had on him. Checking it was loaded, he pointed the barrel toward the door and when the other man walked in Dad shot him in the head as if it was one of the infected. He dropped instantaneously. He was dead. I screamed out, I was in shock. Dad dropped the gun and threw his arms around me. He told me that it could very well have been us lying dead on the floor now, that they had wanted our food, drink and weapons and without them we would have been dead anyway. I helped Dad to drag both of the men's bodies outside. Dad drove their car away from the house too, and he found alcohol and gasoline in the car and even 2 hand grenades which he brought back into the house.

We had secured the place once again when we heard a noise coming from outside, I went with Dad to investigate. It was the man that Dad had strangled. He was one of them now, he was a walking corpse and he was trying to get in. I shot him before Dad had the chance, he'd done he's fair share of saving us for one day. I missed the head on the first shot, the gun was heavier and harder to control than I had anticipated. I kept firing at him, a bullet hit his chest but he just kept on walking, then I hit the target and he fell to the floor. We talked for hours about how he had turned into one of them, Dad checked his body for bite marks but found nothing, and this freaked us all out. Mr Brafhail was more concerned that the TV had now stopped broadcasting anything. Now we are just waiting, waiting for help, waiting for the infected to find us, waiting for looters to try to take what we have, but most of all, we are waiting for answers. We now live in hope.

Kerry N. Smith

Found Voice Recording in Salem United States of America — person unknown.

God help me please.

It's too late for me now. I've been bitten and know I'm infected with this virus. No one knows what caused this, but all of us know what happens when you get bitten or infected. I've seen people turn in an instant – but for some people it takes longer. It seems the weaker, or people with health problems, turn quicker, as if their immune system can't even try to ward off or fight the virus.

I've been infected for two minutes. My right arm is where I've been bitten. It's numb and tingling, it feels like my arm is on fire. I suppose I'm a coward. I've seen people chop of limbs just to try to stop the virus spreading. But not all have been successful. Some are too late, and some just die anyway, in more pain. I think the virus is somewhat mutating. It takes only a few minutes for people to become infected. I've no feeling in my arm now at all. The bite's too high – I would have to chop the whole arm off. I've nothing to remove my arm with. The water I'm drinking tastes like acid. My feet are now tingling and I can't stop shaking. I don't want to die! I've let everyone down, myself and my family.

This whole journey has been wasted. I was trying to get back to my family from town, but there were just too many of the infected. They're slow and even if you find yourself amongst crowds, you can mostly go around them. Though they seem to lunge forward and get quicker if they see meat in sight. The meat being us, the ones who are not infected "yet." The infected don't feed from each other and I've seen them walk straight past animals. I think the other survivors are maybe more of a threat than the zombies; it's not just me who thinks this. Everyone's changed. I've been shot at by kids as young as nine years old and threatened with knives for my belongings, for what good they were. I hid my water in my pants. Water is the most precious commodity now.

The shakes are getting worse. My eyes are blurry and feel like they're burning and I'm sweating and it's hard to breathe. I'm going to pass out any second. I've no energy. My head feels like I'm dying from the inside out, like a hot poker has just been pushed through my head. I'm clammy everywhere. I'm so hot! The water won't go down, my throat's closing. It's getting harder to talk. I can't move my neck now. My body feels like it's on fire! Ahh! Why me God? Why?

I can do this!

Gunshot fired.

Live UK Radio interview — Originally Broadcast October the 10th 2019.

"Good evening.

"Tonight I'm talking to Doctor Marzeal who has kindly given up his time to come in and do this interview for us, here at 365 Live News.

Doctor Marzeal, what is causing this?"

"At this moment we're still unsure as to what has actually caused the virus. We know it's spreading at a rapid rate, and the initial symptoms are very similar to standard influenza symptoms."

"Is this a terrorist attack? Can we expect there to be further incidents?"

"At present we don't believe that this is an act of terrorism. But we do predict more outbreaks. However, at the moment, we need to focus all our resources on controlling this one."

"Is there a vaccine?"

"Not as this stage, but governments have been in talks with scientists and global pharmaceutical manufactures, and have an experimental vaccine ready and are working hard to get it out there for public use. Of course, we don't want to take any short cuts and end up doing any more harm. It's a delicate balance between getting the vaccine out there, while leaving enough time to determine any other side effects from taking the vaccine itself.

"I know for certain that, even as we're speaking, there are a team of scientist's working day and night on getting this right and getting a safe and effective vaccine into production and out to the public at large. "

"Did you ever think we would see the dead actually walking and attacking people?"

"Not in a million years! This thing is nothing short of horrific. You couldn't imagine this in your wildest nightmares."

"Anyone who has the infection, or should I say, the second stage, the rabid rage. Are they officially dead already? Is there any way of coming back from this?"

"Firstly, yes, once someone enters the second stage, they're as good as dead. The hope is that there will be a way in the future to bring them back. The numbers of second stage patients is rising by the second. There are tests being carried out to try to find a way to reverse the apparent neurological damage and reclaim people. We're currently looking at this as a form of coma – where there are signs of life, there is some hope. "

"What are the government doing to contain this?"

"The government are working around the clock and using every means at their disposal for the safety of the public. Quarantine is in place all over the United Kingdom, Scotland and Wales and safe zones are being set up as quickly as possible. As of now we have no plans for evacuating the United Kingdom. But, in this unique situation, that may be subject to change. All public transport has been suspended. We're asking for everyone to try and remain as calm as they possibly can and to have the utmost respect for the law".

"What's the virus called?"

"The virus has the name of H15-z1 that's what we're presently calling it. We've never encountered anything like this previously. Something that has the ability to travel at such a rate."

"Why wasn't this contained sooner?"

"The infection spread at such an uncontrollable and unpredictable rate. The government tried its best and still is. This is now a war that we're all trying desperately to win. We're losing members of our precious police, fire and air rescue, along with the military. We haven't seen anything like this, with this kind of capacity for devastation, since World War II. All I can say is, we just weren't prepared for a virus that could spread so rapidly."

"What should the public do to stay safe?"

"There's a strict protocol in place. It'll vary from area to area.

If you're in a town or a city, you'll be removed and ushered to a safe location. We're advising people to leave their homes in densely populated locations, such as busy towns and cities, for their own safety, but at no point will anyone be forced out. Please bear in mind that we have everyone's safety and care as our first priority.

Since the start of this emergency, I've seen people risking their lives going back to unsafe zones to collect their phones, or TVs, photo albums. This kind of action places lives at risk. Please leave any belongings behind.

"If you're in an area where the advice is to stay indoors, then lock all the doors and windows. Board them up where you can, and only open the door to a government official. This is for your own safety. If you're in a position at home where you can safely boil your water before drinking it, then please do so. We don't believe that the water is currently contaminated, but this is just a precaution".

"There are reports that the virus has spread all over the world."

"At this moment there have been numerous reports that other countries have the virus. I can't say any more than that. These are only reports."

"Doctor, I'm very sorry but we've just been informed that we have to cut this interview short and evacuate the building immediately."

"What—?"

"Oh my God no…"

End of Broadcast.

Notes found in Central London.

I am documenting my own personal experiences since this crazy virus outbreak on 10th October 2019 in order that any possible survivors or future generations may ascertain and get some kind of clarity in piecing together how and what went so wrong.

When the news broke our office was evacuated. I've never seen anything like it before. Panic was setting in as hordes of people desperately tried to escape the dangers of the city. My initial thought was to make my way home but as I approached the station I stared in shock as people rushed down the steps and into onto the platform. People were getting squashed and trampled on whilst others screamed and shouted, pushed and shoved, desperate to try to board the tube. Everyone had a look of terror in their eyes. I changed my plan! Then I heard someone shouting, telling people to go back. I heard whistles being blown; the tube and, I was later to discover, all public transport had ceased operation. It would only have taken one of the infected down there in the underground, just one in that close proximity, with no way out. It was tantamount to signing your own death warrant. I was with some colleagues and we headed in the opposite direction.

Heavily armed police were ordering people off the streets, and advising people to find somewhere safe to wait it out. We didn't have anywhere safe, the only place we knew in the area was our office, so we quickly decided to head back there. There were four of us and once back inside Lucas and I took the heaviest things we could find (desks, copiers and chairs) and dragged and piled them in front of the doors and windows. Everything had changed in an instant – we had found shelter – but we were far from safe.

The kitchen fridge was fairly well stocked, so we knew we'd have food supplies for a least a few days but then we started to run low. The noise the infected made was relentless; the guttural sound coming from them was enough to turn any sane human being crazy. We had no light and the days began to merge into one. The windows were barricaded and we hadn't seen daylight in days, the darkness only served to intensify the fear and loneliness.

It didn't take long for us to turn on each other. It was inevitable really, our primal instinct as human beings is to survive and a few days into being holed up things took a turn for the worse. We had already gathered all the makeshift weapons we could find, so we were armed (in a very loose sense of the word), but we were anything but prepared for what happened next. We were sleeping when it happened. We all woke up to the sound of an almighty crash as the glass from one of the larger windows collapsed. Mere seconds later they were inside. Leona slept nearest to the window, she was first to be infected. I was no hero, I didn't pretend to be. I was frozen with fear. It seemed as though the world around me was running in slow motion as the two other guys stopped them dead in their tracks. I was right to stay the hell away though – all three of my former colleagues were bitten. The window was swiftly boarded up again, but I was trapped, knowing that these people could turn at any moment. Lucas (the tough guy of us all) killed the others before they had a chance to turn. He tried to hide the bite wound on his arm from me but I knew it was there and I knew what I had to do to survive…

I had no choice…

I no longer recognize myself. It's not my reflection in the mirror. My eyes don't resemble the person I once was. My eyes are now soulless. Outside of these doors, society has crumbled, whilst inside, all that's left is a shadow of the person I used to be.

There's very little food left here I still have electric and I'm boiling the water from the water dispenser before drinking it. The last three days have felt like an eternity, I'm a sitting duck, waiting to starve to death, or waiting to get infected or attacked.

How long can I stay here for?

Is help going to come or will I die here?

Will I come back as one of the infected dead?

Will I become a zombie?

Dean Torrenze 23

Hand written notes found in Michigan October 10th 2019.

My name is Alex Cohagen. I live in Michigan, and I have worked as a doctor here and studied medicine since I was able to read. My curiosity for medicine and this profession comes from my father who was also a doctor. As a child, I would sit alone in my father's study, just staring at the full size skeleton he kept in there and studying the diagrams on the posters covering the walls. Friends would occasionally ask me if a human could actually turn into a zombie. To be honest, I didn't put my thoughts into the matter – apart from at dinner parties, when I would normally make something up, just to see people's reactions. I would play devil's advocate saying, yes, it could happen. But I never imagined we would actually come to this. I am lucky enough to, so far, be free of this terrible plague. Since it took hold, I have placed all my energies into trying to determine the possible cause. It's not brain parasites, it's not a neurotoxin. I'm beginning to think, due to the nature and effects, that CJD could be a possible cause, or at least a partial one.

CJD: Creutzfeldt-Jacob-Disease is basically a form of brain damage that will lead to a quick decrease of movement and will affect, mental function. Normally you would be looking at one or two cases per a million people. This is a very rare disease. CJD is most commonly known as Mad Cow Disease and can be contracted only by eating infected meat. Looking at the reports in the media, we first received information of an influenza type infection that combined with cannibalistic tendencies. Most of the initial reports were from foreign countries – mostly hot places that would have acted like an incubator for the virus. Then, very quickly, we began to get mass reports of a flu virus. Collating the information, we see a list of symptoms that look very similar to a recent pandemic – flu, including swine flu.

Then, in a matter of hours, there are reports of further symptoms: sudden jerking movements or seizures, muscle stiffness, lack of coordination, blurred vision, dementia and hallucinations. All of which are the same symptoms as would be present with CJD or VCJD, mad cow disease.

In some countries they are calling this cattle flu, so there could easily be a connection to cattle. Who knows – we could have been eating infected meat. Does this mean vegetarians will be OK? No – at the rate this virus is travelling no one is safe. The more I search, the more I become convinced that there must be a connection to mad cow disease. It is just too much of a coincidence. H5N1, avian flu was a very wide spread virus but was comparatively weak when compared to other widespread pandemics. We can rule out aids and avian flu unless H5N1 has mutated. Ebola, although a very severe virus, is not as easily contracted and could not spread as fast. I am therefore ruling ebola out! H7N9, bird flu is transmissible to humans, and there is also a possibility of a mutation of this virus. I can't fathom the uncontrollable rate at which it spreads and the symptoms it causes in those infected are like nothing we have ever seen before. Tamiflu and Relenza have been used to effectively treat H7N9 but have had no discernible positive influence against this virus to date.

I know it's early days but time is most certainly not on our side in the fight to safely control the spread of this virulent disease. The infection must break the blood-brain barrier to cause the symptoms which we have seen. It is uncommon for a standard influenza, or even a bite, to spread infection to the brain. Breaking the blood-brain barrier at the rapid rate of this virus is unheard of. The brain itself is the only organ to have its own unique security system, capable of stopping foreign bodies, and this is being broken down in minutes, when infection would be expected, in the normal course of events, to take weeks, if not months to reach the brain and break this down. The so-called zombie virus is spread by close contact to the infected or through coming into contact with their blood or saliva, and most usually as the result of being bitten. A single bite, as from someone infected with rabies, is known to have a longer incubation period before it breaks down the blood-brain barrier, but this thing would appear to attack it instantly. I find myself in a position of total confusion. The virus, at every stage, would seem to indicate that the patient has been in contact with, or been a carrier, for a very lengthy period. Does this then indicate that we all carry the virus – or at least a form of it? If so, then the assumption must be that being exposed to either the full-blown virus in someone who is infected, or being bitten, triggers the onset of the disease. This could be a mutation of the influenza virus, or cattle flu, or perhaps CJD? However, the unnatural speed with which the stages take place and the rate of spread defy anything naturally occurring and lead me to suspect that this is some man-made variant.

We are only a few hours into this pandemic – who knows what is to come next? I pray this is not...

The End

Notes

Notes

Notes

Notes

If you prefer to spend your nights with Vampires and Werewolves rather than the mundane then we publish the books for you. If your preference is for Dragons and Faeries or Angels and Demons – we should be your first stop. Perhaps your perfect partner has artificial skin or comes from another planet – step right this way. Our curiosity shop contains treasures you will enjoy unearthing. If your passion is Fantasy (including magical realism and spiritual fantasy), Horror or Science Fiction (including Steampunk), Cosmic Egg books will feed your hunger.